Kidnapped in Key West

Kidnapped in Key West

Edwina Raffa and Annelle Rigsby

Pineapple Press, Inc.
Sarasota, Florida

Inquiries should be addressed to:

Pineapple Press, Inc.
P.O. Box 3889
Sarasota, Florida 34230

www.pineapplepress.com

Library of Congress Cataloging-in-Publication Data

Raffa, Edwina.
Kidnapped in Key West / Edwina Raffa and Annelle Rigsby. -- 1st ed.
p. cm.
Summary: In 1912 in the Florida Keys, twelve-year-old Eddie Malone's father is falsely accused of stealing the Florida East Coast Railway payroll and Eddie sets out with his Labrador retriever, Rex, on the trail of the real thieves. Includes historical notes about the Keys and the construction of the "Over-Sea Railroad."
ISBN 978-1-56164-413-1 (hardcover : alk. paper)
[1. Robbers and outlaws--Fiction. 2. Florida East Coast Railway--Fiction. 3. Railroads--Florida--Fiction. 4. Labrador retriever--Fiction. 5. Dogs--Fiction. 6. Kidnapping--Fiction. 7. Florida Keys (Fla.)--History--20th century--Fiction.] I. Rigsby, Annelle. II. Title.
PZ7.R4435Kid 2008
[Fic]--dc22

2007040417

First Edition
10 9 8 7 6 5 4 3

Printed in the United States of America

Contents

FLORIDA 1912

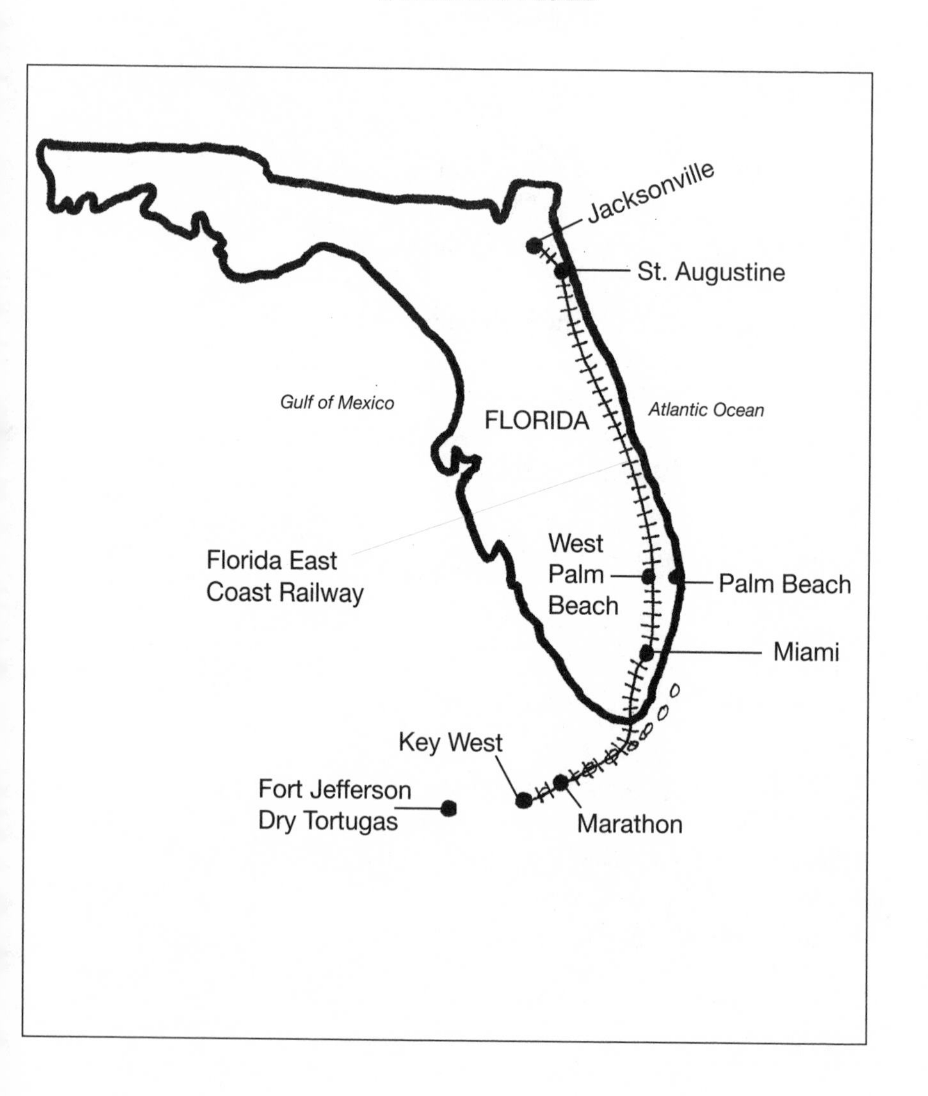

THE MIDDLE AND LOWER FLORIDA KEYS

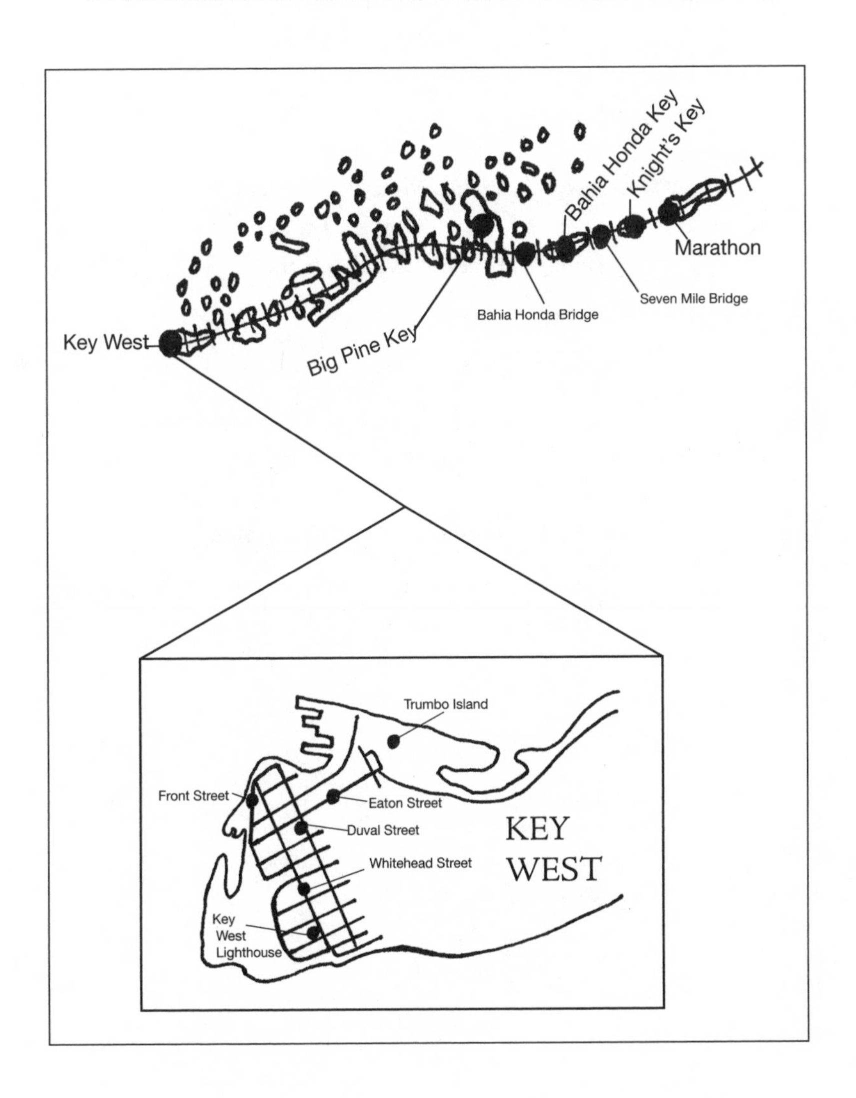

To my grandchildren, Ashlynne, Brinson, Tess, and Benjamin,
for the many happy hours we've spent together reading books.
—Edwina

To my wonderful husband, Mike Rigsby, with love and
heartfelt thanks for the countless times you have
generously shared your talents.
—Annelle

The authors would like to thank Holly Hughes, Education
Director of the Henry Morrison Flagler Museum in Palm Beach,
Florida, for checking the historical facts in this book.

1

Trouble in Marathon

January 1912

"You're in big trouble, boy!" growled Frank Malone. The burly railroad worker stomped the mud from his boots in the doorway of the Florida schoolhouse and glared at his son.

Twelve-year-old Eddie Malone glanced up at his father from the blackboard where he was writing one hundred times "I will not skip school." He quickly lowered his blue eyes and nervously pulled at the cowlick in his red hair. Then he went back to his punishment.

Frank Malone was not in good humor. Being called from the job to meet with his son's teacher meant missing half a day's work. These days, all railroad employees were expected to work around the clock. Henry Flagler's Key West Extension had to be finished in a week so the famous tycoon could make his ceremonial ride to Key West. Frank looked grim as he removed his straw hat and crossed the rough plank floor to meet with Miss Inez Brown, Marathon's schoolmarm.

Miss Brown was a stout middle-aged woman whose face constantly wore a scowl. Her students called her Frowny

Browny behind her back and frequently made jokes about her wide figure when she turned to write on the chalkboard. Now she sat grading seatwork in the back of the one-room school, barely visible over the clutter of papers and books piled high on her desk.

At the sight of Eddie's father, Miss Brown tucked a loose strand of gray hair into her bun. She dabbed the perspiration on her neck with a lacy handkerchief and straightened the belt around her thick waist.

Miss Brown greeted Eddie's father and motioned him to a chair across from her. Then she swiveled around to get the attendance record behind her on the bookcase. As she strained to reach the top shelf, the seam of her sleeve made a ripping sound. The pink flesh of her upper arm popped out like a sausage from its casing.

"Oh, my!" exclaimed Miss Brown, momentarily flustered. She hastily snatched the record book and then reached for the shawl draped on her chair. After wrapping it around her shoulders, Miss Brown sat with her arms clamped stiffly against her sides.

A nervous snicker started at the back of Eddie's throat. He bit his tongue to stifle it. He had already dug himself into a deep hole of trouble and laughing at the teacher now would be disastrous. Instead, he fixed an earnest look on his face as he continued to write and listen in on the adults' conversation.

"I'll get right to the point," said Miss Brown, peering sternly at Frank Malone over her wire-rimmed glasses. Her look dared him to mention the ripping incident and even Frank Malone's toughness evaporated under such scrutiny.

"Eddie's failing because he's missed too many lessons. He *must* come to school every day or he will repeat seventh grade!"

Eddie's eyes widened in alarm. He cringed in spite of himself at Miss Brown's dreadful warning.

Uh-oh. I'm in for a switching and now that Pa knows I've been skipping school, there'll be no more fishing for me.

Eddie stole a glance at Pa who was looking down at his calloused hands, roughened by shoveling marl at the pit. Then Pa looked up at the teacher.

"I apologize for my son's behavior, Miss Brown," he said. "To tell the truth, I ain't been supervisin' him real close. You see, Eddie's ma died back in Jacksonville not long ago and we've been goin' through some bad times. When I took on this job with the Florida East Coast Railway, or F.E.C. as we call it, I thought Marathon would be a good place for Eddie. I know schoolin' is important but he really likes to fish and swim."

"School comes first," said Miss Brown firmly. She pursed her lips for emphasis. "Eddie *must* be here every day."

"I'll try to see to it," he said, "but we've been workin' night and day to finish the railroad extension. A week from Sunday, a survey train will be sent to Key West and back to test the tracks. Mr. Flagler's countin' on us to be finished by then."

"I sure want Eddie to get schoolin'," Frank Malone continued. "Eddie's ma wanted that too. She always made sure he done his lessons and spoke good English. Someday I'd like him to get a desk job, not one fightin' mosquitoes and diggin' in the marl pit like me. Buildin' up roadbeds for them tracks is gruelin' work."

Miss Brown sighed. "Yes, well, please talk to your son, Mr. Malone. A boy's father can be a tremendous influence."

"Yes, ma'am," agreed Frank Malone standing up. "I'll do that."

Then turning to Eddie, he said, "When you finish them

sentences, git on home to your chores. I'm headin' back to work, but make no mistake, when I git home tonight, we'll talk."

Frank Malone jammed his straw hat on his head and strode out the door. Eddie knew what "we'll talk" meant. Most likely, Pa would give him a good switching for skipping school.

After finishing up sentences ninety-nine and one hundred, Eddie waited impatiently for his dismissal. Finally Miss Brown glanced at the clock on the wall and waved him out. Freed at last, Eddie burst out of the schoolhouse into the bright sunshine of the Florida Keys.

"Come on, Rex," called Eddie. A big yellow Labrador retriever was waiting patiently in the shade of a buttonwood tree. At the sight of his master, he sprang to his feet and wagged his tail happily.

Eddie bent down to pat Rex's head and whispered, "Pa won't be home till late. Let's go on over to Matthew's house. There's plenty of time to finish my chores before Pa gets home."

Whenever Eddie needed a friend, he would walk over to see Matthew Lawrence. Matthew was a kind old man from the Bahamas who lived in Adderley Town, the small black community in Marathon. Before retiring, Matthew had worked as a carpenter for the Florida East Coast Railway and he liked entertaining Eddie with stories about the railroad.

When Eddie first came to Marathon, Matthew had taken him under his wing. The old man owned a small sailboat that he used when harvesting sponges to sell in Key West. Matthew had taught him how to sail the boat and sometimes let him borrow it to go fishing.

Eddie threw sticks for Rex to fetch as he walked along

the sandy path to Adderley Town. When they arrived, Matthew was resting under the gumbo limbo tree near his white concrete house. The green wooden shutters at the windows were propped open, letting in a cool breeze.

"Hey, Matthew. How are you?"

"I'm doing all right," said Matthew. "How about yourself?"

Sheepishly, Eddie confided in his friend about his trouble at school.

When he finished, Matthew said sympathetically, "I know you'd rather be outdoors, but you need book learning too."

"Yeah," sighed Eddie. "It's just more fun to catch fish than to memorize poetry."

Matthew smiled and said, "You've got that right."

"Can you go fishing with me now?" asked Eddie.

"Sorry, but I'm weeding the garden today. My melons and squash need more room to grow," said Matthew, "but you're welcome to take the sailboat out by yourself."

"Thanks," replied Eddie. "I'm going to fish over at Sand Dollar Key."

"Sounds good," said the old man. Then looking up at the sky, he added, "Just keep your eye on the weather. My achy bones tell me a storm is brewing in the Gulf."

Eddie whistled for Rex and hurried toward the dock where Matthew's sailboat was tied. Rex hopped in first and sat straight up on his haunches ready to catch the wind in his ears. Eddie picked up a fishing pole that leaned against the mangroves. Then he jumped in behind Rex and set sail for his favorite place to fish and swim.

The fish weren't biting so Eddie anchored the boat offshore. He pulled off his shirt, kicked off his shoes, and dove into the clear, blue water. Rex jumped in after him and paddled around. When Eddie surfaced he took a deep breath and plunged deeper to search for horse conchs on the coral reef. Schools of tiny yellow and blue striped fish darted past him as he dove again and again.

The sun had dropped low in the western sky when Eddie realized that once again he'd lost track of time. Quickly he returned the sailboat to Matthew's dock and ran home with Rex. It was nearly dark by the time he reached the camp where all the new railroad employees and their families lived. As he approached his tent, Eddie saw Pa's muddy boots by the screen door.

"Uh-oh, Pa's home and my chores aren't done," said Eddie, holding Rex back by his collar. "We'd better stay away and give Pa time to cool off."

With his devoted companion at his side, Eddie ambled through the dusty, deserted streets of Marathon, killing time until he could go home. As he slapped at mosquitoes that bit his arms, he was glad it was January and not summertime. He'd heard the mosquitoes were so thick in the summer months they looked like black curtains covering the window screens.

He and Rex continued to wander the roads until they came to the water tower by the railroad tracks. As Eddie looked up toward the top, a full moon slipped out from a bank of dark rain clouds.

"Stay, Rex," ordered Eddie. He began to climb the rungs of the tower's ladder, tasting and smelling the salty sea air as he went. When he reached the top, he sat down and let his legs dangle between the rails. Marathon spread out below him like a picnic cloth on the ground and the whole town was quiet. Eddie watched the lights in the men's dormitories go out one by one as the exhausted railroad workers turned in for the night.

Looking down from the tower, Eddie could see the paymaster car parked at the Florida East Coast Railway station. He knew that tomorrow hundreds of hard-working railroad men would line up to receive their wages in gold coins. They had come from many different countries to fill the ranks of workers Henry Flagler needed to build his Over-Sea Railroad.

Then Eddie noticed his pa's supervisor, Mr. Tate, out on his nightly stroll. When he looked more closely, he saw Pa coming from the opposite direction. Frank Malone waved to Mr. Tate as the two men passed in the road.

Eddie hoped Pa would walk on by. At that moment, however, Rex spotted Pa too and let out a friendly bark to greet him. Frank Malone stopped, then stepped back away from the water tower and looked up.

"I see you, Eddie," he called. "Git on down here."

Eddie began to climb down very slowly. He needed time to think of a good excuse for disobeying Pa.

Maybe if I point out the paymaster car and remind Pa that tomorrow is payday, he'll get in a better mood and forget about the switching.

When Eddie reached the bottom, he stood silently before his father. Frank Malone raised his eyebrows, clearly waiting for an explanation. Seeing his father's serious look, Eddie decided to apologize.

"I'm sorry, Pa," said Eddie. "I went fishing and lost track of time. I should have done my chores like you said. Are you going to punish me?"

Frank Malone paused for a minute to consider the situation. Then to Eddie's surprise, Pa didn't punish him. Instead he put an arm around Eddie's shoulders.

"No, son," he said. "I guess you've had enough for one day. When you wasn't at the tent, I was right worried."

"I know you've had to fend for yourself lately," he continued. "And I wish things was different, but I'm doin' the best I can . . . I need you to do your best too."

Eddie looked up at his pa and replied solemnly, "I'll try, Pa. I really will."

Just then a flash of lightning lit the sky and a roll of thunder rumbled in the distance. "Me and you better move along," said Pa looking up at the threatening clouds.

Eddie called to Rex and the three started back just as the skies opened up and a winter rain began to fall. As they crossed the tracks to reach their camp, Eddie suddenly stopped.

"There's a light moving inside the paymaster car," said Eddie pointing down the tracks. "What do you think it is, Pa?"

Frank Malone turned and looked toward the paymaster car.

"Might be trouble," said Pa. "You go on home while I take a look-see."

When Eddie and Rex got back to the tent, they were soaking wet. Eddie dried himself off and then dried Rex. After hanging the towel neatly over the indoor clothesline, he wearily crawled into his cot and covered himself with a blanket. Rex curled up on the floor beside him and soon the two were fast asleep.

Just as the early morning light crept into the camp, Eddie was awakened by a booming voice outside their tent.

"Frank Malone, come out in the name of the law!"

2

Thieves

The sheriff's loud voice sent Rex into a barking frenzy. Eddie and Pa sprang from their cots in alarm. While Pa pulled on his boots, Eddie tried to calm Rex down but it was no use. Rex sensed danger and he continued to bark.

Rubbing sleep from his eyes, Frank Malone hurried to the tent's screen door and looked out. Eddie held Rex back, but the dog kept growling and straining at his collar. Finally Eddie let Rex pull him towards the doorway to stand beside Pa.

Charlie Jenkins, Marathon's sheriff, and Mr. Tate, Pa's supervisor, stood in the yard. It was still drizzling from the night before and rain dripped off their hat brims.

"Get out here, Malone," ordered the sheriff. "I need to speak with you . . . and shut that dog up!"

"What's wrong, Pa?" asked Eddie. "Why are Sheriff Jenkins and Mr. Tate outside?"

"Nothin' I can't handle," answered Frank Malone. "Keep Rex quiet while I go out and see."

"Yes, sir," said Eddie, leaning down to get a better grip on

Rex's collar. Then Eddie tried to soothe him by scratching the dog's ears as he eavesdropped at the doorway.

"That's the man I saw last night running out of the paymaster car," said Mr. Tate, pointing directly at Pa.

"Are you sure?" asked the sheriff.

"Positive," answered the supervisor. "Frank Malone works for me down at the marl pit."

"I didn't do nothin' wrong," protested Frank.

"I saw him there, Sheriff," insisted Mr. Tate. "Do your job."

Sheriff Jenkins took a step closer to Pa. "Why don't you and I go into your tent and have a look around."

Eddie pulled Rex away from the door to let Pa and Sheriff Jenkins inside. Mr. Tate stood guard on the steps.

After a brief search, the sheriff asked skeptically, "Well, Malone, what did you do with the payroll?"

"I'm tellin' you, Sheriff," said Pa, sweat breaking out on his forehead, "two strangers done stole it."

"Were you in the paymaster car last night?" questioned the Sheriff impatiently.

"Yes, I seen a light and . . ."

Before Pa could finish, Sheriff Jenkins impatiently interrupted. "So you admit you were there?"

"Yes, but I didn't . . ."

The sheriff wasted no time. He quickly pulled a set of handcuffs from his pocket and clapped them onto Pa's wrists. "Frank Malone," said Sheriff Jenkins firmly, "you're under arrest for robbing the F.E.C. payroll."

The sheriff forced-marched him outside and the three men started towards the jail. Eddie left Rex in the tent and ran after the sheriff.

"You can't take Pa away," blurted Eddie, grabbing on to the lawman's sleeve. "He's no thief. This is a mistake!"

The sheriff brushed Eddie's hand away. "Sorry, boy," he said, "but I've got a job to do."

Eddie ran over to the railroad supervisor. "Mr. Tate, my pa would never steal. He's an honest man!"

"I know what I saw," said Mr. Tate gruffly. "Maybe your pa will remember what he did with the payroll after cooling his heels in jail for a while. Now, go on back to your tent. This is grown-up business."

"Eddie, do what Mr. Tate says," said Pa, trying to keep his voice strong. "I'll git this mess straightened out directly."

Eddie had no choice but to obey. He went back to the tent and sat down on the edge of his cot to think. He was scared for Pa and for himself too. Rex padded over and put his head in Eddie's lap. He whimpered softly and looked up soulfully at his master.

"Pa's in big trouble, Rex ol' boy. What are we going to do?"

Eddie stroked Rex's head absentmindedly as he tried to come up with a way to help Pa, but it was no use. He just couldn't think on an empty stomach.

"I guess we'd better get some breakfast, Rex. Then let's go over to Matthew's house."

At the word breakfast, Rex's tail began to thump the floor. He yipped a couple of times and Eddie could have sworn that Rex was smiling. After running a comb through his unruly red hair and splashing water on his face, Eddie called to Rex. Together, they left the tent and headed over to the dining hall.

Eddie left Rex at the door and entered the building alone. The dining hall was crowded with railroad workers who sat shoulder-to-shoulder at long, wooden tables, wolfing down their first meal of the day. He recognized one of the marl pit workers who had the same shift as Pa.

"Hey, boy," the worker yelled, "where's your pa this morning?"

Eddie pretended not to hear. He just wasn't up to telling the man about Pa's arrest so he hurriedly moved to the food line.

The cook handed him a plate of eggs, ham, and biscuits. Eddie put it on his tray and took a seat by himself in the corner. He toyed with his eggs for a few minutes, moving them back and forth across his plate. Finally, he gave up. He stuffed the biscuits in his pocket and left the building.

Outside, Rex was waiting patiently as usual. Eddie stooped down and fed his Lab the biscuits. Then they started toward Adderley Town. Along the way, Eddie passed several of his schoolmates playing catch. He gave them a half-hearted wave, but ignored their invitation to join the game. As he approached Matthew's place, Eddie saw Matthew's wife. She was cooking in the kitchen house, a small building built behind the main house like ones in the Bahamas.

"Looking for Matthew?" she called out. Eddie nodded. "He's in the garden. Go on around."

As soon as Matthew saw the droop in Eddie's shoulders, he put down his hoe. "Something on your mind?"

Eddie nodded. "I . . . I . . ." He couldn't finish his sentence.

"Go sit in the shade," said Matthew. "I'll make us a pitcher of limeade. I just picked some Key limes this morning and a cool drink would taste good about now."

Eddie sat on a chair under the gumbo limbo tree and watched Matthew cut open some small, greenish-yellow limes and squeeze the juice into a pitcher of cool water. Then the old man sweetened the juice with sugar cane and poured it into two tall glasses. He handed one to Eddie and set the other on the small table beside his chair. Before he sat down, Matthew thoughtfully put a bowl of water on the ground for Rex.

The limeade was delicious, but neither his favorite drink nor relaxing in the shade could relieve Eddie's fears. He took a deep breath and let out a sigh.

Matthew reached over and patted Eddie's arm. "Take your time. I'm in no hurry."

Eddie took another deep breath and then began talking. Once he started, it was easy to pour his heart out to his trusted friend. Matthew listened intently to every word about the sheriff's early morning visit and Pa's arrest.

When Eddie finished, he glanced hopefully at Matthew. "What should I do?"

The old man looked squarely into Eddie's eyes. "Well, for now there's nothing you can do. Why not stay here a while? Mrs. Lawrence is just about ready with breakfast. Then later, after the sheriff sorts things out, you can go over to the jail and see your father."

Eddie felt the heaviness in his heart lift a little. He could always count on Matthew for practical advice.

Eddie's appetite returned as the aroma of frying fish wafted from the kitchen house. When Mrs. Lawrence called out, "Breakfast is ready. Come and eat!" he jumped up and followed Matthew inside.

While Rex napped under the tree, the Lawrences and Eddie sat around the wooden table eating fried flounder along with the pineapple and cantaloupe from Matthew's garden. For the first time, Eddie tried "hurricane ham," the Bahamian name for dried conch. It was chewy, but good. When they finished, Mrs. Lawrence got up to clear the table. As she passed behind Eddie, she put her hand on his shoulder.

"Eddie," she suggested, "get Matthew to tell you a railroad story while I put things away. That'll take your mind off your troubles."

Turning to Matthew, Eddie asked, "Would you tell me one?"

Matthew smiled widely, showing several gold-capped teeth. Besides fishing, there was nothing he liked better than talking about the railroad. The old man ran his hand several times over his white, close-cropped hair while he decided which story he'd share.

"Have I told you about the hurricane of nineteen-oh-six?" he finally asked.

"No," replied Eddie. "I'd like to hear about it."

That was all the encouragement Matthew needed and he launched into his story.

"After Mr. Flagler built the Florida East Coast Railway from Jacksonville to Miami," began Matthew, "he decided to extend the line on down to Key West. Train tracks had to be built across one hundred and twenty-eight miles of coral reef and ocean floor. To keep construction on schedule, we had to work during September and October, the worst months for hurricanes.

"That worried me a lot because hurricanes are dangerous and unpredictable. That's why I always carried this little barometer."

Matthew reached into his pocket and pulled out a small glass tube filled with water. A weed was floating in the bottom of it.

"Many railroad workers carried these and checked them as often as they did their watches. I still like to keep mine handy."

Matthew went on to explain, "When the air pressure goes down, the weed rises. That means a hurricane is coming and you'd better get ready.

"About six years ago, I was working on the Long Key viaduct north of here making cofferdams. Those are the wooden forms that mold the cement foundations for the bridge. Well, at any rate, on the evening of October seventeenth, when I checked this tube, the weed was moving up. I was living on a houseboat then along with one hundred and sixty or so other railroad workers. The houseboat was tied down so it couldn't drift off, but that night the wind got stronger and the waves got higher. Pretty soon, the houseboat started rocking back and forth something fearful."

Matthew paused for a moment to collect his thoughts, then continued, "The next morning, the hurricane hit us full force and the houseboat's cable snapped in two. I'll never forget the terrified screams of the men as they were tossed into the water when the houseboat broke apart. I grabbed onto a wooden plank floating by. Believe me, I clung to it like a tick to a dog. I floated for hours until finally the hurricane was over and a passing freighter rescued me.

"When I got back to Long Key, I couldn't believe the terrible damage to the bridge. Most of our hard work was wiped out. We had no choice but to start all over again. After the houseboat accident, Mr. Flagler ordered the construction of new dormitories on land and living in those made us feel much safer.

"Yes, Eddie, what with the hurricanes of nineteen-oh-six, nineteen-oh-nine, nineteen-ten, and the construction accidents, building the Key West Extension has been a tough job. Many men have given their lives to build Mr. Flagler's Over-Sea Railroad, but thanks to workers like your father and me, it is almost finished. Why in just a little more than a week, Mr. Flagler will finally achieve his goal of connecting the U. S. mainland to Key West by rail."

The old man fell silent. He looked off in the distance, as if the story had transported him back in time.

"Wow," said Eddie. "That was some adventure. I'm sure glad you lived to tell it."

Matthew's attention snapped back to the present and he stood up to stretch. "So am I, Eddie, so am I. Well, I've kept you long enough. You're probably anxious to be on your way."

Eddie nodded and got up from the table. After thanking the Lawrences, he and Rex hurried through town to the jail. Eddie left Rex at the screen door and went inside.

The sheriff was tilted back in his chair with his hat pulled over his face taking a snooze.

"Ah-hum," said Eddie, pretending to clear his throat.

The sheriff sat up and quickly put his hat back on his head.

"What do you want, boy?" asked Charlie Jenkins.

"I'd like to see my pa," said Eddie.

"I reckon you can visit him just this once," said the sheriff, getting up from his seat and unstrapping a ring of keys from his belt. "Come with me."

Eddie followed the sheriff along a narrow hallway that reeked of stale sweat. When the lawman reached Pa's cell, he stopped, opened the door, and let Eddie inside. Then he locked it again.

Frank Malone sat on the sagging mattress of his cot, listlessly peeling flakes of gray paint from the walls. Like prisoners before him, he'd found that it was a way to pass the time. He paid no attention to the cockroach crawling across his boot.

Seeing Pa locked up in such a bleak place made Eddie

sick to his stomach. His hands began to tremble and he quickly clasped them behind his back so Pa wouldn't see how scared he was.

Pa?" asked Eddie timidly.

Frank Malone stood up and gave his son a weak smile. His voice cracked a little when he spoke.

"I ain't got no money for bail so they've locked me up till they can schedule my trial."

"Trial?" asked Eddie. "Why are they having a trial? What happened last night?"

"After I told you to go back to camp," explained Pa, "I went into the paymaster car to see about that light. I seen the safe door partway open, so I grabbed the handle and checked inside. It were empty.

"Then I heared a noise outside the back door. I walked out onto the platform and seen two men runnin' off with the payroll bags. I chased 'em to the dock, but by the time I got there, they was already sailin' off toward that favorite fishin' hole of yours.

"Them robbers got away, but I seen their sailboat. It had a navy blue jib on it. I wanted to tell the sheriff, but he weren't nowhere around. By then it was rainin' buckets so I jist gave up and came on home."

Pa's eyes took on a frightened look as he continued, "Now Mr. Tate, he claims he didn't see no other men. Just me. Eddie, he thinks I done stole the F.E.C. payroll! What's worse, my fingerprints is all over that paymaster car."

"Aren't the thieves' fingerprints on the doors too?" asked Eddie.

"No, they was wearin' gloves," said Pa. "I tried telling the sheriff all this, but he wouldn't listen."

"This is all my fault!" cried Eddie, his eyes welling up with tears. "If I had stayed home and done my chores like you told me, you wouldn't have been out searching for me and we wouldn't have seen that light!"

"It ain't your fault, Eddie," said Frank Malone. "It's just the breaks."

"They'll match your fingerprints to the ones in the paymaster car," said Eddie. He shut his eyes tight and pressed his fists hard against them to stop the tears.

"I'll cross that bridge when I come to it," said Pa. "Now stop cryin' and git on home. Remember, this ain't your fault."

Eddie hesitantly took a step toward Pa. Then he wrapped his arms around his father's waist and buried his face in Pa's shirt. Pa patted his back a few times, but said no more.

It was the hardest thing Eddie had ever done, but he finally let go of Pa and stepped away. Then he wiped his nose on his shirtsleeve and called to Charlie Jenkins.

The sheriff took his own good time coming. He opened the door and escorted Eddie out, immediately locking the cell behind him.

Eddie walked slowly outside to get Rex, guilt still gnawing at his heart. No matter what Pa said, Eddie felt responsible. He trudged home with Rex at his side, oblivious to the rain that soaked him to the skin.

When Eddie entered the tent, he could tell right away that it had been searched. The two cots were in the middle of the floor and the trunks that held their clothes had been ransacked. Even some of the floorboards had been pried up. Pa was right. Sheriff Jenkins wasn't buying Pa's story one bit and had checked the tent from top to bottom.

Eddie thought about straightening things up, but he was just too tired. He kicked off his wet shoes and fell into bed. He pulled the blanket over his head and soon the rhythm of the rain on the canvas roof lulled him to sleep. Rex jumped up on the cot and kept his faithful watch all through the night.

* * *

The next day was Sunday and Eddie awoke to golden sunshine in a cloudless blue sky. He felt clearheaded after a good night's sleep and his brain was simmering with a plan. He talked out loud to Rex while he put the tent back in order and changed his clothes.

"I need to borrow Matthew's boat," he said when he finished. "Come on."

Along the path to Adderley Town Eddie bumped into the Lawrences on their way to church. He asked Matthew about the sailboat.

"Sure, take it," said Matthew. "I won't be using the boat today."

Soon Eddie and Rex were sailing east toward Sand Dollar Key. Eddie had a hunch the thieves' sailboat might be in the small cove there. Obscured by mangroves, it would be the perfect place to hide. Sure enough as Eddie steered into the cove, he saw the sailboat with the navy blue jib. Men's voices floated over the morning stillness from the center of the little island.

"Come on, Rex," said Eddie, pulling the boat onto the beach. "Follow me."

Eddie walked a hundred feet inland. Then he crouched down and peeked through a clump of saw palmetto. Two men were packing canvas bags into crates marked *Key West Coffee Company*. Eddie moved in a little closer and parted the palmetto fronds to get a better look. Each bag was stamped with the F.E.C. logo and the word *Marathon* on it.

My hunch was right! This is the thieves' hideout!

"Now that the rain's let up, Bart," said a short, wiry-looking man, "we can sail on down to Key West."

"Right you are, Leo," replied a bearded man with a deep, raspy voice. "We'll just stash these gold coins with the rest of the loot. Why, this is the easiest robbery we've pulled yet and the best part is that some pit worker is in jail for our crime." He grinned through rotten teeth.

Suddenly the dry palmetto frond Eddie was holding back snapped. The startled robbers looked up from their work.

"Who's there?" yelled Bart, racing directly toward Eddie's hiding place.

Eddie tried to stand up and run, but before he could move, a hand gripped the collar of his shirt and lifted him off the ground.

3

Key West Bound

Eddie wildly punched the air with his fists and kicked his legs in every direction to break free, but his efforts were in vain. The thief was as strong as a giant. He just tightened his viselike grip on Eddie's collar and shook him like a dust mop. Finally Eddie was able to croak, "Sic him, Rex!"

The obedient Lab made a flying leap from the bushes, knocking Eddie and Bart to the ground. As Rex lunged at Bart again, Eddie rolled away from his grasp and scrambled to his feet. Rex growled and bared his teeth, holding the thief at bay. Then he charged and latched onto the man's pants, sinking his sharp teeth into Bart's long, fleshy leg.

"Yeow!" howled Bart, writhing in the sand. "Leo, don't just stand there, help me!"

The skinny man picked up a stick and cautiously edged forward. Rex let go of Bart and chased after Leo. The little man dove into a nearby coffee crate and quickly pulled the lid over it.

"Good boy," called Eddie. "Let's get out of here!"

Clutching his bloody leg, Bart made a feeble attempt to chase Eddie, but he couldn't keep up the pace. Eddie and Rex darted back to the boat and Eddie pushed off from the beach as he jumped in. His courageous dog was right behind him. The little boat's sail quickly caught the wind and Eddie steered toward home.

After docking the sailboat, Eddie and Rex raced straight to the jail. When they got there, Eddie leaned against the building for a minute to catch his breath. Then he opened the screen door and stepped into the front office. This time Rex came too.

Charlie Jenkins was reading a newspaper at his desk. He lowered it slightly to glance at Eddie. He frowned at Rex.

"I found the thieves!" gasped Eddie.

"What are you talking about?" asked the sheriff with a yawn.

"Two men with the payroll!" blurted Eddie. "They're on Sand Dollar Key."

Eddie told Sheriff Jenkins about discovering the two thieves and watching them hide the payroll bags in crates marked *Key West Coffee Company*. Then he explained how he and Rex had narrowly escaped.

"Come with me right now," urged Eddie, "and I'll show you the *real* thieves!"

Charlie Jenkins grinned and chuckled to himself. "My goodness, boy, I haven't heard such a good yarn in a coon's age."

"But it's true," Eddie insisted. "I really did see them!"

The smile quickly slid from the lawman's face and an impatient look filled his eyes. "Look, boy. You come in here and tell me a wild tale about some robbers. What you don't have is concrete proof to back your story, do you? Well, do you?"

Eddie slowly shook his head.

"Didn't think so, but I do," said Sheriff Jenkins. He spoke in an odd singsong voice as he stated the facts of the case to Eddie. "Frank Malone was seen running from the paymaster car. Frank Malone's fingerprints match the ones on the safe. Frank Malone's fingerprints match the ones on the doors. As soon as I find where he's hidden the money, Frank Malone will be convicted because Frank Malone *is* the F.E.C. payroll thief."

"You're wrong about Pa," said Eddie angrily. "He's not a thief and I'll prove it."

"I'd like to see you try," taunted the sheriff. "In the meantime, take your dog and get out of here."

"At least let me go back there and tell Pa," pleaded Eddie pointing to the jail cells.

"No," Sheriff Jenkins replied sternly. "There's no more visiting hours before the trial. Now, go!" He picked up his newspaper again and began reading.

Eddie slowly walked to the office door. He pushed it open and he and Rex left feeling more disheartened than ever. It had never occurred to him that the sheriff would doubt his story.

"I guess it's just as well that the sheriff didn't go to Sand Dollar Key," said Eddie to Rex. "With my luck, by the time he got there, those crooks would be long gone."

"Oh, Rex," he said sadly. "I really messed up and now Pa has to pay the price."

As Eddie walked toward the camp, he turned the recent events over and over in his head. He had to find a way to get Pa out of jail. Suddenly, Eddie stopped and squatted down nose-to-nose with Rex.

"I've got an idea, Rex. Sheriff Jenkins said I have no concrete proof and he's right. I don't. But if we go down to

Key West and find the Key West Coffee Company, then we'll find the stolen payroll. I just know it. Bart said that's where they stash all their loot.

"If I can just get one of those payroll bags then I could take it to the Key West police. A payroll bag with *Marathon* stamped on it should be enough evidence to make the police investigate the Key West Coffee Company. Then they can arrest the real thieves and Sheriff Jenkins will have to free Pa. Do you think my plan will work?"

Rex barked once and then licked Eddie's face.

"Good ol' boy," Eddie said as he stood up. "Now let's go home!" Without wasting another minute, they ran back to the camp.

That afternoon Eddie sat on the steps of the tent and thought carefully about what he was going to do. Then he talked the plan through with Rex.

"We'll go to Knight's Key in the morning," he said, "and catch the *Montauk*. It's a steamer that picks up Marathon passengers heading for Key West."

Rex cocked his head and listened attentively.

"We'd better travel light because we have a long way to walk and besides, we don't want to attract attention. In the meantime, we should act natural so nobody suspects we're up to something."

At suppertime Eddie went over to the dining hall. He took an extra portion of roast beef for Rex and put two rolls in the pocket of his knickers. Back at the tent, he fed Rex the tasty meat. Then Eddie picked up the bucket and went to get water. Since there was mostly salt water in the Florida Keys, large cedar barrels of fresh water had to be loaded onto flatbed cars and shipped down by train. Several water barrels were nearby so Eddie didn't have to lug the full bucket too far. When he returned to the tent, he set aside some drinking water and then used a little for washing.

At dusk, Eddie lit the lantern. He shut the tent flaps over the windows to keep out the cool winter air and then amused himself by making shadow monsters on the canvas. When he grew tired of playing, he just lay on his cot and stared at the ceiling. Eddie sure missed Pa, even his snoring. As if sensing his master's loneliness, Rex pushed his soft, furry head under Eddie's hand.

"Don't worry, boy," said Eddie, scratching the dog's head. "We'll be all right as long as we stick together."

The next morning was Monday, but Eddie didn't go to school. He should have, considering all the trouble skipping school had caused him, but Eddie had other plans. He was on a mission to free Pa and he was determined to get started.

Eddie put on his jacket and stuffed his savings of two dollar bills, three quarters, five dimes, and a nickel into his pocket. Then he and Rex set out for Knight's Key to catch the *Montauk*.

The January morning was cool and a steady breeze was blowing off Boot Key Harbor. Eddie buttoned up his jacket and quickened his steps as he and Rex walked along the train tracks toward the small island just below Marathon.

Suddenly the shrill sound of a train whistle blew behind him, announcing the approach of the train bringing water to the Keys. Eddie grabbed Rex's collar and the two jumped off into a patch of weeds that grew alongside the tracks. They watched as old work engine No. 10 roared by, spewing black smoke from its coal burner into the clear Florida air. When the clickety-clack of the train's wheels finally passed, Eddie and Rex climbed back onto the tracks to continue their trek to Knight's Key.

At last Eddie caught sight of the Knight's Key dock. The *Montauk* was already there loading passengers. With Rex loping behind, Eddie ran out to the end of the long dock where the deep Atlantic waters swirled around its pilings. Men and women bound for shopping in Key West and vacationing in Cuba jostled each other as they boarded the steamer.

Eddie and Rex crowded in with a group of noisy children who were traveling with a well-dressed lady and gentleman. The two adults chatted with another couple who also had several children in tow. No one seemed to notice an extra boy and his dog joining the rowdy youngsters.

Once the *Montauk* was under way, Eddie and Rex stood with the two families at the railing watching the Florida scenery go by. As the steamer slipped past Pigeon Key, Eddie could see a large crew feverishly working on the tracks in the middle of the Seven Mile Bridge. He knew they were trying to finish in time for Mr. Flagler's inaugural trip the following Monday.

As they passed the Bahia Honda Bridge, Eddie counted thirty-four concrete piers. Pa had told him that the steel trusses had to be brought in by barge to construct the trestle bridge. He'd also said the Bahia Honda Channel had been the most dangerous section to build across because of its strong currents and deep water. When Rex began to whine and edge under the railing, Eddie quickly pulled him back. He knew how much Rex loved water, but this was not the place for his Labrador retriever to go for a swim.

The crystal-clear water fascinated Eddie too. From his place at the railing he could see a coral reef that had taken thousands of years to grow. It was made from skeletons of tiny sea animals called coral polyps, which looked like large branches under the ocean. A hammerhead shark cruised through a hole in the coral and purple sea fans waved in the tropical currents. Several bottlenose dolphins playfully followed them for miles, arching through the water that churned behind the boat.

As they passed Big Pine Key, Eddie strained to see the tiny Key deer that inhabited the island. Suddenly a young boy next to him spotted one and started shouting. He jumped up and down and pointed in the direction of Big Pine Key.

Immediately a crowd formed around Eddie and Rex. People leaned heavily on the railing trying to catch a glimpse of the shy Key deer. Suddenly the railing cracked under the combined weight of so many passengers and started to rock dangerously back and forth. People screamed. Mothers reached for their children. Some people panicked and started pushing.

"Move away from the starboard side," ordered the captain.

Eddie held onto Rex's collar while he struggled through the crowd until they finally broke free. Shaken by the near accident, Eddie sank down on a bench and hugged Rex. Several crew members arrived on the scene and herded the rest of the crowd away from the starboard deck. As soon as it was cleared, they roped off the section of the damaged railing until it could be fixed in port.

"You almost got that swim you wanted, Rex, ol' boy," said Eddie, "and I almost got a really close look at that Key deer."

Then after a moment of thoughtful consideration, he added, "We could've drowned and never gotten back to Marathon. No one even knows where we are. Maybe I should have told Pa I was going to Key West, but it's too late now."

Rex answered with an understanding bark and licked Eddie's hand. Then Eddie reached into his pocket and took out the two rolls from last night's supper. As he and Rex ate their meager meal, Eddie started to smile.

"About now old Frowny Browny is reading poetry to the class," said Eddie. "I'm sure glad we're here instead."

It was almost dark when the *Montauk* pulled into Key West. Eddie was tired and he could tell the other passengers were too. It had been a long trip and the near mishap had drained everyone's energy. Eddie followed the other children as they pushed and shoved their way down the gangplank and on into town.

Once Eddie reached Duval Street, he began looking for a place to spend the night. An old hotel with weathered clapboards caught his eye. A faded sign hanging over the front porch read "B'tween Waters Hotel—Meals Included."

"Maybe we could afford that place," he said to Rex. "Let's see."

Rex trotted behind Eddie as he entered the lobby of the shabby hotel. They crossed a carpet so worn it was impossible to tell what its original color had been. An old woman with frizzy hair and a wrinkled face looked up from behind the desk.

"What do you want?" she asked rudely.

"We need a room," answered Eddie.

"Where're you from, boy," she asked, "and how long do you plan on staying?"

"I'm from Marathon," said Eddie, "and I just need a place for tonight."

A greedy gleam sprang into her squinty brown eyes. "Do you have any money?" she asked.

"Yes, ma'am," said Eddie pulling out the savings from the pocket of his jacket. He laid the money on the desk so he could count out the correct amount.

Quickly snatching up all of Eddie's money with her gnarled fingers, the woman said, "Well, this'll cover room and board for you. Your dog stays outside."

"But we're together," insisted Eddie. He tried to sound grown up despite the quiver in his voice.

"Health Department rules. No dogs in the hotel," the landlady said abruptly. "Your room is on the left at the top of the stairs."

Eddie sighed and bent down to explain to Rex.

"Just for now, Rex," he whispered very softly, "I'll come get you later and sneak you inside."

Eddie led his dog outside to the huge royal poinciana tree beside the hotel.

"Stay, Rex," he ordered. Rex whimpered once and then lay down. He put his head between his paws and sadly watched Eddie go back into the B'tween Waters.

"Can I have something to eat?" Eddie asked when he was at the desk again.

"Meals come with your room," said the woman. "Go in the kitchen. Pedro will give you supper."

Eddie found the kitchen and sat down at the table. A short man with a huge smile handed him a plate of deep fried grunt fish and sweet potatoes.

"*Aquí está tu comida,*" said the cook. Eddie had heard a little Spanish in Marathon and knew that meant "here's your meal." Then the man handed him two biscuits and added in a low voice, "*Para tu perro.*" Eddie smiled as he knew this was for Rex.

Eddie took the plate gratefully and gobbled down the food. When he was finished, he crossed the lobby and started up the front stairs toward his room. On the landing, Eddie paused at the window to check on Rex. As he stood there, he could hear the landlady downstairs talking to two men.

"Welcome back, gentlemen," she was saying. "Your room's waiting for you."

"Thanks," answered one of the men. "Sure will be good to have a soft bed and some of Pedro's vittles. He's the best cook in town."

"Where'd you go this time?" asked the landlady.

"We had to deliver some coffee to Marathon."

"Hmmm," said the woman, tapping her cheek with her fingertip. "A young 'un with hair redder than a Key West sunset and his big yellow dog came in here tonight. He said he's from Marathon. I suspect he might be a runaway. I gave him the room at the top of the stairs, but I'm keeping my eye on him."

Suddenly the other man spoke up. "You don't say! Marathon! Why me and Leo ran into a real troublemaker in Marathon that meets that description."

Eddie froze in his tracks when he heard the familiar raspy voice. It was Bart! He listened more intently.

"A troublemaker?" asked the landlady. "I run a clean establishment here. I don't want anything to do with a troublemaker."

"Don't you worry none, ma'am," said Bart. "Me and Leo will go upstairs right now and check on the lad for you. If he's who we think he is, we'll get rid of him pronto!"

4

The Lighthouse Children

Eddie threw open the window on the landing and crawled out onto the ledge. He squinted into the darkness, searching for a way to escape. Then he saw it. A sturdy pipe used to channel rainwater ran from the roof into the cistern below. Without a second to spare, Eddie leaped onto the pipe and slid down like a fireman. When he got near the bottom, he jumped off and rolled onto the grass.

"Come on, Rex," shouted Eddie scrambling to his feet. "Let's go." At his master's command, the yellow Lab jumped up and followed.

Bart's gravelly voice at the window yelled after him. "Halt there, boy. I want words with you."

Eddie ran blindly through the dark street with Rex at his heels. He couldn't tell if the sound he heard was the thud of boots chasing him or just the pounding of his heart. He looked over his shoulder once and sure enough, Bart and Leo were following close behind. He increased his speed.

Up ahead, Eddie spied two brick buildings with an alley

running between them. He ducked into the narrow passageway and sprinted toward the light at the end, looking for a place to hide. When he found the recessed doorway of a cigar factory, Eddie grabbed Rex and pulled him into the shadows. He wrinkled his nose against the pungent odor of tobacco that oozed from an open factory window.

"Stay quiet, Rex," ordered Eddie. He wrapped his arms tightly around the dog's neck and hissed, "No barking!"

A minute later, Eddie's heart skipped a beat as he watched Bart limp by with Leo tagging close behind. Rex struggled to break free and chase them, but Eddie kept a firm hold on the Lab's collar. Together, they waited until Eddie could no longer hear the thieves' footsteps. Then he relaxed his grip on Rex and stroked his back.

"That was a close one, Rex," whispered Eddie. "Those are dangerous men. They're glad Pa's in jail. Bart and Leo think they're safe from the law, but they didn't count on us, did they?"

Eddie sank down onto the wooden frame of the doorway and rested his back against the door. Rex curled up next to him and began nuzzling at his pocket.

"Oh, yeah," said Eddie as he fished the biscuits out of his pants, "thanks for reminding me. These are for you."

Rex took a biscuit in his mouth and put it between his paws. He gnawed contentedly while Eddie outlined his plan.

"We'd better stay here for tonight. First thing tomorrow morning, we'll find the Key West Coffee Company. Then we'll stake it out . . ."

Eddie's eyelids began to droop and before he could finish his sentence, he was asleep.

Tuesday morning Eddie woke up stiff after spending

the night in the cramped doorway. He stood and stretched his arms over his head to loosen his muscles. Rex was still asleep, small pieces of biscuit still clinging to his whiskers.

"Wake up, boy," said Eddie gently shaking his friend. "We've got to get out of here before the factory workers come."

Eddie and Rex left the alley and wandered back down Duval Street in the opposite direction of the B'Tween Waters Hotel. Eddie had heard about Duval Street from Matthew Lawrence. It was known as the longest street in the United States because it started at the Atlantic Ocean and ended at the Gulf of Mexico. Eddie noticed that all the stores along the street were draped with red, white, and blue bunting and flying American flags. The two-story houses were decorated island-style with palm fronds and coconuts tied on the porch railings. When he passed a book store, Eddie paused in front of its large display window.

"Would you look at that, Rex!" exclaimed Eddie.

The shop owner had set up a miniature train layout of the Over-Sea Railroad. A toy train ran on tracks that crossed over little bridges.

"This model is just like the real railroad, only smaller . . . like we're up in a Wright flyer looking down on it."

At that moment, a shop clerk stepped out of the store with a broom in his hand. He started sweeping in front of the store.

"That's some display, isn't it?" said the man. "I just put it in the window yesterday for the big celebration."

It seemed to Eddie that everywhere he looked, people were getting ready for "the big celebration." He couldn't get involved in that though. He had more important things on his mind, like locating the Key West Coffee Company and finding the stolen F.E.C. payroll.

"It's swell," agreed Eddie. "By the way, could you . . ."

"Yessiree," interrupted the talkative clerk, "come next Monday, the whole town will be full of people. Everyone's ready to celebrate the arrival of the first train to Key West. Why it was only two years ago when the first spike was driven here to start construction at this end. Now, in less than a week, the crossover span at Knight's Key trestle will be closed and the tracks will be ready. The famous railroad tycoon, Mr. Henry M. Flagler, is coming here in person and he'll be bringing a *trainload* of business to this town. . . . Get it, a *trainload* of business?"

Eddie forced a polite smile at the shopkeeper's attempt at humor. All he wanted was directions to the coffee company, but the man wouldn't let him get a word in edgewise. With a wave goodbye, Eddie and Rex moved on.

After walking the length of Duval Street, Eddie and Rex turned back and started looking for the coffee company along some of the side streets. One short street ended in front of a sprawling banyan tree. The tree had numerous trunks and its branches had roots growing from them down to the ground.

Next to the banyan tree was a white brick lighthouse that rose over eighty feet into the air. A wooden house with a porch running along three sides stood nearby. The chicken coop, well, and cistern were behind it. A picket fence ran around the entire lighthouse grounds. The front gate had been left open.

Eddie watched as two children about his age stepped out onto the wide porch of the house. They sat down on the floor to play a game of dominoes. Just then, a rooster strutted in front of Rex. Immediately the dog bounded inside the gate after it. The ruffled rooster flapped its wings and flew toward the coop. He landed on the roof and let out a shrill crow.

"Come here, Rex!" shouted Eddie from the gate. "Leave that rooster alone!"

The boy and girl left their game and trooped down the porch steps laughing.

"Don't worry," said the brown-headed boy as the youngsters approached the gate. "Your dog will never catch old Lightning. He's the fastest rooster in Key West."

The boy was right. The three children watched as Rex whined and paced back and forth near the chicken coop. Lightning just stretched his neck out and crowed again and again.

"Sorry," apologized Eddie. "I'll get him and be on my way."

"Oh, don't worry about Lightning," said the pretty girl with dimples and long, brown braids.

"I just didn't want Rex to get him," replied Eddie. "By the way, my name is Eddie Malone. What's yours?"

"I'm Jen Kimble," replied the girl, "and this is T. J., my twin brother. We live here at the Key West Lighthouse. Our mother, Martha Kimble, is the lighthouse keeper."

"Your mother's a lighthouse keeper?" asked Eddie.

"Yes," replied Jen. "When our father died, she took over. But we all work to keep it running."

"My ma died last year," blurted Eddie. He wondered how that fact had popped out so quickly to perfect strangers. Maybe it was Jen's sweet face or the interested way she looked at him. It really didn't matter. He knew he'd found a friend. Eddie smiled at her and watched her dimples return when she smiled back.

"Where are you staying?" interrupted T. J. impatiently.

"Well, I haven't found a place that will take my dog and besides, I'm out of money."

"Are you all by yourself?" asked Jen, concern in her eyes.

"I've got Rex," answered Eddie confidently. "We'll be fine."

"Are you a good diver?" asked T. J.

"Yes," said Eddie. "Why?"

"There's a big cruise ship in port this morning," said T. J. "Tourists throw coins from the ship's deck and watch the locals dive for them. It would be a quick way to make some money. I'd go with you, but I've got school."

"Thanks, T. J.," said Eddie. "I'll give it a try."

While T. J. gave Eddie directions to the ship, Jen picked up the dominoes and put them away. Then a woman's voice came from inside the house. "You two better get on to school now."

"Yes, Mother," Jen called back. "We're on our way."

"We've been practicing songs for the big celebration for two straight weeks," Jen explained to Eddie. "We're going to sing in a chorus with one thousand children."

She opened the screen door and called, "We're leaving now, Mother. Bye."

"Come on, Jen," said T. J. pulling one of her braids. "Let's go."

As the twins started running down Whitehead Street, T. J. turned around and yelled, "Good luck with the diving, Eddie. Come on back here after school and tell us how you did."

"We'll be at the banyan tree," shouted Jen.

Eddie and Rex watched until the twins turned the corner. Then he headed toward the docks. Eddie was amazed at the size of the ship he saw anchored there and the number of tourists on board lining the railings. Two older boys already stood poised on the dock, toes curled over the edge, ready to dive.

"*Aquí está una moneda de plata!*" yelled a Cuban man, holding up a silver coin. He motioned Eddie to join the two who were waiting to dive.

"Stay, Rex," Eddie ordered. Stripping off his jacket, shirt, and shoes, Eddie raced to stand beside the older boys. The three watched as the man tossed the coin.

Eddie hit the water first. He could see the silver dollar slowly float down through the cold clear water toward the bottom. Kicking his feet with all his might he dove deeper and snatched the coin just before it disappeared into the white sand.

"I've got it!" Eddie shouted, holding the silver dollar high above his head as he burst through the surface of the ocean waters. He swam furiously to the edge of the dock and grabbed the extended hand of a smiling fisherman who pulled him onto the wooden planks.

"*¡Tú eres un bullidor magnífico!*" called the Cuban man from the ship.

"What'd he say?" Eddie asked the fisherman as he scrambled onto the dock.

"He said you're a magnificent diver." His weathered face broke into a grin as he slapped Eddie's back in a congratulatory gesture. "But what does that tourist know? He throws his money away!" The man laughed heartily at his own joke.

Eddie and Rex sat on the dock and watched the other boys dive. When he was dry, Eddie put his clothes back on. Then he and Rex headed for the stores that lined the waterfront, following the enticing aroma of frying conch fritters. It led them to a small eatery between two cigar stores. Eddie went in and placed his order.

Saliva dripped from Rex's mouth onto the dirt street as he sniffed the smell of fried food in the air. When Eddie came out, he put three conch fritters on the ground for Rex. Then he sat down next to his dog to eat his own fritters, always watching for Bart and Leo.

"We've got to find that coffee company, Rex," mumbled Eddie between bites.

As he ate, Eddie looked up and down the waterfront searching for its sign. No building in sight gave any clue that it was the Key West Coffee Company. When Eddie finished eating, he licked the fritter crumbs from his fingers and wiped his hands on his pants.

"Come on, Rex," said Eddie. "Let's go see what's in those buildings over by the docks. Maybe the coffee company is there."

When he reached the first building, Eddie saw a man with a clipboard supervising a construction job. Eddie walked over and said politely, "Excuse me, sir. What's going on here?"

"We're working on Mr. Flagler's train terminal here on Trumbo Island."

The man made a dramatic sweep of his arm. "Mr. Joseph Parrott had thousands of cubic feet of mud and marl pumped from the bottom of the Gulf to make this ground. We Conchs figured he was digging up half the bay, but I guess he had to do it. Land here in Key West is pretty scarce."

"What's in the buildings?" asked Eddie.

"Well," answered the supervisor, "in addition to the terminal, there are a few stores and warehouses."

"Do you know if the Key West Coffee Company is in one of them?" asked Eddie hopefully.

The man scratched his head and thought. "Can't say that I've ever heard of it, but we've had several new companies move in. You're welcome to walk around and look. Just keep your dog out of the workers' way. We've got a deadline to meet."

"Yes, sir," promised Eddie. "I will."

When he had checked every store and warehouse, Eddie sat down to rest under the awning of an outdoor market. Gradually he became aware of an unpleasant odor. Looking around he discovered a display of sheepswool sponges in a nearby stall.

"Eeww! Those sponges stink!" said Eddie to the yellow Labrador. "Let's go back to the lighthouse, Rex. Maybe Jen and T. J are home from school by now."

Eddie and Rex walked slowly back to Eaton Street, then turned onto Whitehead Street and followed it to the lighthouse. When they got there, he didn't see Jen and T. J. at first. They sat high up in the banyan tree hidden in the large branches that covered the side yard and backside of the lighthouse.

"Eddie," called Jen through the branches, "We're here. Come on up."

Leaving Rex at the bottom, Eddie climbed the tree and joined Jen and T. J.

"You look like a monkey!" said Jen, flashing her dimpled smile.

"Speak for yourself," teased Eddie. "All you need is a banana."

"Did you go diving?" asked T. J.

"Yes, and I got enough money to buy Rex and me some food," said Eddie proudly.

"Eddie," said Jen unable to contain her curiosity a second longer, "why are you in Key West by yourself?"

Eddie made a quick decision to trust the twins. He needed help and he needed it fast. He started at the beginning and told them everything, about the payroll robbery,

Pa's arrest, and even his plan to find the Key West Coffee Company to prove Pa's innocence.

"Gosh!" exclaimed T. J. "That's some story!"

"I'm so sorry," said Jen. "What can we do?"

"I don't really know," said Eddie. "I don't want you to get in trouble."

"We'll think of something," said Jen with convinction.

"Yeah," echoed T. J. "We'll think of something."

The twins and Eddie sat in silence for several minutes but no one came up with any good ideas. Finally T. J. said, "Let's play marbles. Maybe something will come to us later."

"Now there's an idea," said Jen. "Let's go!"

The three friends climbed down the banyan tree and walked over to the path leading to the twins' house. Eddie drew a circle in the dirt while T. J. and Jen went inside to get their bags of marbles. When the twins returned, T. J. set up the game and Jen gave each one a shooter. Then the three began to play.

Suddenly from the corner of his eye, Eddie caught the movement of two figures coming towards them. When he looked up, he saw Bart and Leo heading their way!

5

Night in the Lighthouse

"It's those thieves!" exclaimed Eddie, pointing down Whitehead Street.

Sure enough, Bart and Leo were prowling through the neighborhood, stopping to check each house. They were definitely looking for someone and that someone was Eddie Malone.

"Quick, Eddie, call Rex and run to the lighthouse," whispered Jen. "Take the stairs up to the first landing. Crawl into the alcove there and hide until T. J. and I come get you."

"Don't worry," added T. J. "We'll handle this."

Eddie jumped up and whistled to Rex. The two ran across the yard to the entrance of the lighthouse. Quickly, Eddie pushed the door open and they slipped inside.

The lighthouse was shaped like an ice cream cone turned upside down and a circular iron stairway ran up through its center. Late afternoon sunlight filtered down through windows at the top, casting shadows from the branches of the banyan tree outside.

Eddie grasped the railing and started climbing. His footsteps echoed with a metallic sound as he moved rapidly up the circular staircase. After a few seconds of climbing, Eddie paused to catch his breath.

I hope Jen and T. J. are all right. I don't want Bart and Leo to hurt them because of me.

Suddenly Eddie realized that Rex was not behind him. He leaned over the spiral railing and looked down. Rex was whining and walking back and forth at the bottom of the stairway.

Cupping his hands around his mouth, Eddie called softly, "Come, Rex, come."

Rex tentatively put his paw onto the first step.

"That's the way, Rex," urged Eddie. "You can do it."

Encouraged by his master's words, Rex slowly worked his way up the stairs until he reached Eddie.

"Good boy," said Eddie, giving his dog a pat. "Now follow me."

As they wound around, they passed an open window. A thick limb of the banyan tree was growing right up to it. The limb was so close Eddie could have touched it. When he and Rex reached the landing Jen had described, they both crawled into the alcove and waited.

After a few minutes, Eddie heard footsteps on the spiral stairway. He held Rex close to his side. When he saw the faces of the Kimble twins, Eddie let out a sigh of relief. He let go of Rex and they both crawled out from their hiding place.

"What happened?" asked Eddie.

Both twins wanted to talk at once, but they took turns as they often did when telling a story.

"Bart and Leo walked up to us while Jen and I pretended to be playing marbles," explained T. J. "Then one of the men, Bart, I think, said they were looking for a red-headed boy . . ."

" . . . and that he'd seen one with a dog running through the yard," continued Jen.

"So Jen thought quickly," said T. J. "She said . . ."

"I said, 'You must have seen our tomboy sister, Gladys with our dog, Leroy. She was playing marbles with us until our mother called her inside.'"

Jen smiled, obviously pleased with her quick response to Bart's question.

"Did he believe you?" asked Eddie.

"Well," admitted T. J., "the short man, Leo, did ask if we were sure about that . . ."

" . . . so I answered firmly, 'No offense, Mister, but I think we know our own sister when we see her,'" said Jen with a laugh. "That seemed to satisfy them."

"At least we hope it did," added T. J., a bit of doubt creeping into his voice.

"Thanks for helping me," said Eddie. "Now I still have a chance of getting the proof I need."

Jen looked over at her twin brother. "Maybe we should tell Mother about this."

"No, Jen. We can't do that," said T. J. "If we told Mother, she'd take Eddie straight to the police and they'd send him home before he finds the payroll. Without proof, the Key West police won't believe him . . ."

" . . . and act just like the Marathon sheriff did," sighed Jen. "You're right, T. J. We'd better keep this to ourselves, at least for now."

"In the meantime," said T. J., "Eddie needs a place to stay."

"Why can't he stay right here in the lighthouse?" suggested Jen.

"Good thinking, Jen," said T. J. "He should be safe up here."

Jen turned to Eddie and said, "You can hide out in the alcove. Then tomorrow, we'll go with you to look for the coffee company. With the three of us searching, I'm sure we'll be able to locate it."

"I hope so," replied Eddie. "I need to find that stolen payroll as soon as possible. Are you sure it'll be all right for me to stay here?"

"It'll be fine," said T. J. "We just need to keep Mother from seeing you, but that'll be simple enough. Jen can tell her I'm lighting the lantern tonight."

"Won't your mother be suspicious?" asked Eddie.

"No," T. J. answered. "Since we turned twelve last November, Mother lets us light the beacon all the time. After all, working in the lighthouse is a Kimble family tradition."

"Since Eddie's staying," said Jen, "let's give him a tour of the lighthouse."

Eddie told Rex to wait while he and the twins climbed the rest of the way to the top. Rex, who was obviously not fond of stairs, put his head down between his paws for a nap on the landing.

When they reached the observation platform, Eddie remarked, "That's some climb. Exactly how many steps are there?"

Jen and T. J. exchanged an amused glance. Then the twins answered in unison, "Eighty-eight."

Eddie laughed. "I guess you've been asked that question before."

As the three friends stepped out onto the circular platform, the evening sea breeze whipped their hair and snatched at their clothes. The island city of Key West looked like a big patchwork quilt below them. Houses and shops of all different colors were squeezed together on dirt streets that crisscrossed the island. Eddie located the train terminal near the docks. Then as he moved around the platform, he spotted Duval Street.

When he looked to the west, he could see the Gulf of Mexico's calm, blue waters. To the east, white-capped waves danced on the surface of the mighty Atlantic Ocean.

"Amazing," said Eddie, "and definitely worth the eighty-eight-step climb."

"We think so, too," responded Jen. "T. J. and I come up here at least once a day, especially at sunset. We always look for the green flash."

"What's that?" asked Eddie.

"Sometimes a green glow appears above the sun just as it drops below the horizon," answered T. J. "It's good luck to see the green flash."

"I could use some good luck," said Eddie. "Maybe we'll see it tonight."

"Maybe," said T. J., "but the weather conditions have to be just right."

It was Eddie's first visit inside a lighthouse and he was intrigued with its structure. He wanted to learn all about it. Eddie smiled to himself. Frowny Browny would be shocked to know that he actually liked learning about things.

"Besides being a great place to watch for the green flash," said Eddie with a grin, "why was this lighthouse built here?"

The twins were always pleased when someone took an interest in their home, especially someone as bold and daring as Eddie. They immediately began to explain.

"The light helps boats navigate through the dangerous reefs," said T. J. "Before the lighthouse was here, lots of ships hit the rocks and wrecked. In fact, salvaging wrecked ships was one of the first businesses in Key West."

Jen picked up the story. "When ships filled with valuable cargo crashed up on a reef, people in town would yell, 'Wreck ashore!' Then wreckers would race out to the damaged ship to rescue the crew and its freight."

"Wow," said Eddie. "There must have been a lot of shipwrecks if salvaging was a business. How long has this lighthouse been here?"

"Since 1847," replied T. J. "It was built to replace one that was blown down during a hurricane. Then in 1858, a third-order Fresnel lens was installed in the lantern room."

"A third-order what?" asked Eddie.

"Come on," smiled Jen, "we'll show you."

Eddie followed the Kimble twins up the narrow steps to a round room made of windows. They stepped out onto the small circular ledge that ran around a huge glass lens. The chunk of glass was so large that Eddie could have walked inside it.

"The lens is over fifty years old and came all the way from France," Jen said proudly.

"It looks like the base of a giant cut-glass crystal lamp," remarked Eddie. "I like the way the light bounces off all the angles."

"Are there other lighthouses in the Keys?" asked Eddie.

"Yes," answered T. J. "There's one about eight miles southwest of here called Sand Key Lighthouse."

"It's built on a sandy reef that's a refuge for terns," added Jen. "Every year thousands of terns build their nests there and lay eggs."

By now the evening sky had taken on the first orange hues of a sunset.

"Sorry to interrupt, Jen," said T. J., "but it's getting late and we don't want Mother coming up here. You'd better take Eddie to the alcove now while I light the lantern. Then tell Mother that I'll be right down for supper."

"All right," agreed Jen. "Come on, Eddie."

Jen led the way down to the alcove. When Rex saw them coming, he wagged his tail happily as though they'd been gone for days. Jen patted Rex while she briefly outlined the evening's plans.

"After we eat, T. J. and I will bring you and Rex some supper. In the meantime, we'll keep a look out for Bart and Leo. I sure hope they've quit searching for you. Well, I'd better get going."

Jen walked down the winding stairs. In a few minutes, T. J. hurried past the landing. "See ya," he called, clattering down the metal staircase.

Eddie crawled into the alcove. Rex followed and curled up beside him.

"We're lucky we met T. J. and Jen," said Eddie as he scratched the dog's ears. "I sure feel better having someone on our side."

A short time later, Jen arrived with a plate of fried chicken, green beans, and cornbread. T. J. brought a big jar of water and a wedge of Key lime pie. As soon as Jen handed Eddie the plate, he began stuffing food into his mouth. Between bites, Eddie pulled hunks of chicken from a leg and fed them to Rex. The twins sat down on the landing and watched them eat.

"This is good," Eddie said, pausing to wipe his lips with the back of his hand. "Thank you."

He knew if Ma had been there, she would have scolded him for talking with his mouth full, but he was so hungry he just couldn't help it.

"Glad you like it," said Jen, laughing at his poor manners.

"Yeah," said T. J. "That's old Lightning you're eating!"

He laughed at the startled look on Eddie's face. "Well, you didn't want Rex to get him, did you?"

"That's not Lightning!" said Jen, poking her twin in the chest with her finger. "He'd be too tough to eat."

"It's good, whoever it is . . . or was," said Eddie taking another big bite off the chicken leg. "In Marathon we eat a lot of fish, but chicken is my favorite."

"We eat a lot of fish here too," T. J. said, "especially lobster and shrimp."

"What about dolphins?" asked Eddie. "You don't eat those, do you?"

"Oh, no!" said Jen. "We call dolphins the angels of the sea. There's a legend about a beautiful bottlenose dolphin named Angelina who lives in the ocean around the lighthouse at Sand Key. If you're ever out in the water and get in trouble, you're supposed to call her name three times. They say Angelina appears from nowhere and saves you by pushing your body to shore."

"Hmm," said Eddie. "Do you believe that?"

Jen reflected for a moment. Then she answered, "Well, dolphins are very smart and extremely friendly, so yes, I think it's possible."

"Well, I don't," said T. J. emphatically, standing up to face his twin toe-to-toe.

"You believe the green flash is good luck," answered his twin staunchly, her hands planted firmly on her hips.

"That's different," argued T. J. "At least I've seen the green flash and you . . ."

Eddie felt responsible for starting the brother-sister argument and he was determined to end it. He quickly interrupted T. J. by changing the subject.

"I've noticed everyone here is getting ready for

Monday's big celebration," said Eddie. "What are you all doing?"

The twins immediately warmed to the new topic. After all, the completion of the Key West Extension was one of the biggest and most anticipated events of the century.

"Well," T. J. said, "we're hanging red, white, and blue streamers from the platform of the lighthouse . . ."

" . . . and of course, we've already told you we're singing in a big chorus to welcome Mr. Flagler, too," said Jen. "You know this one, don't you, Eddie?"

Jen softly began to sing "Yankee Doodle," motioning for T. J. and Eddie to sing along. T. J. rolled his eyes in protest, but the two boys humored Jen by joining in on the chorus.

Rex lifted his head and perked up his ears. Then he joined in too, alternating short barks with long howls. His staccato "singing" could be heard throughout the cylinder of the lighthouse.

"Shhh!" said Jen stopping to quiet Rex. "You're going to give away your hiding place."

"Sorry, Jen," said Eddie. "Whenever Rex hears singing, he joins in. He thinks he's harmonizing."

"Normally, I wouldn't mind, but with Bart and Leo around . . ."

"Speaking of those two," interrupted T. J., "we need to make a plan for tomorrow."

Just then, Rex started whining.

"I think Rex needs to go out," said Eddie.

"We can do that for you," offered T. J.

"Thanks," replied Eddie, "but I'm not sure Rex will climb up the stairs again. He doesn't seem to like heights."

"I know what we can do," said Jen. "After we walk Rex, he can stay in the little tool shed next to the garden. It's just big enough for him and he'll be safe and warm. In the morning, you can get him before Mother goes out there."

"Good idea," said T. J. "Eddie, just be sure to leave the lighthouse before nine o'clock. That's when Mother comes over here to clean the windows and add oil to the lantern."

"Is that all right with you, Eddie?" asked Jen.

"Sure," said Eddie. Then turning to Rex, he instructed, "Be a good boy and go with T. J. and Jen. I'll see you in the morning."

"Don't worry, Eddie," said Jen reaching down to pat Rex. "T. J. and I will take good care of him."

The three friends agreed to meet the next afternoon in the banyan tree. T. J. and Jen said goodnight and helped the reluctant Lab slowly down the metal stairway. Eddie listened to their sure-footed steps tapping on the staircase and out the lighthouse door.

When they were gone, a wave of loneliness swept over Eddie. He huddled next to the wall, trying to keep warm in the drafty lighthouse. The cold January wind made a moaning sound as it blew through the trees outside. The branch of the banyan tree scraped against the wooden shutter below, adding its screech to the eeriness of the dark, empty tower. Somewhere a steeple clock was striking ten o'clock.

Suddenly he heard the lighthouse door below open and close again. Eddie shrank back as far as he could into the cramped space. Footsteps were racing up to the alcove.

When Eddie saw it was only Jen with a quilt in her arms, he heaved a sigh of relief. His nerves had been getting a real workout ever since he'd met Bart and Leo. Eddie's reprieve was short-lived however, when he heard the slow rhythmic thud of heavy boots mounting the staircase.

Jen shoved the blanket into the alcove and pressed her fingers to her lips. Then she pointed upstairs and motioned for him to follow her. They swiftly tiptoed up the stairs and through the door onto the observation platform. As soon as they stepped out, Jen yanked Eddie back against the curved tower wall.

"It's Bart and Leo!" she whispered. "They came into our yard just as I got to the lighthouse door."

At that moment Bart burst out onto the platform.

"That boy's gotta be up here," Bart muttered, "and if he is, I'm goin' to get him. He can't escape this time!"

6

Kidnapped!

Eddie and Jen, their backs flattened against the white brick wall, began edging their way along the lighthouse platform. When they reached the side of the tower opposite the door, Eddie hoped they were safe. Just then he spotted the shadow of Bart coming toward them so he nudged Jen further around the circular platform. Eddie knew if Bart discovered them, there would be no means of escape.

After a few seconds, they heard Bart's grating voice grumbling to himself.

"The boy's not here. I shouldn't have let Leo talk me into this wild goose chase."

Eddie and Jen were afraid to breathe. When they heard the door slam shut, they crouched down on the platform. They both heaved a sigh of relief when they finally saw Bart and Leo leave the lighthouse property.

"That was close," said Eddie in a low voice.

"It sure was," agreed Jen. Her eyebrows knit together in concern. "Do you think those two will be back again tonight?"

"No," responded Eddie. "It's late and they were headed in the direction of their hotel. I think it'll be safe now."

Eddie stood and helped Jen up. As the moon moved out from behind a cloud, it illuminated Jen's pretty face. Her eyes seemed to sparkle in the moonlight.

"Thanks, Jen, for bringing me that blanket," said Eddie, "and for warning me about Bart and Leo. It was swell of you."

Jen blushed at his compliment. "You're welcome." Then she added shyly, "Well, we'd better go. I've got to get back to the house before Mother discovers me missing."

Eddie gallantly opened the platform door for Jen and let her go inside first. It felt good to be out of the winter wind. Silently, Eddie followed Jen back down the stairs until they reached the landing with the alcove.

Jen paused on the landing and said playfully, "Good night, sleep tight. Don't let the bedbugs bite."

"And if they do, I'll take my shoe and beat them till they're black and blue," Eddie promptly answered.

He heard Jen chuckle lightly as she headed downstairs. Eddie darted up to a porthole window and watched until Jen was safely inside her house. Then he went back to the alcove, snuggled down under the warm quilt, and closed his eyes.

The next thing Eddie knew, morning light was streaming into the lighthouse. He'd been dreaming of fishing in Marathon and it took him a second to realize where he was.

After Eddie stood and stretched, he walked up the curved staircase. When he peered out the porthole window, he saw a lady in a long skirt carrying a bucket heading straight toward the lighthouse.

Mrs. Kimble! I've got to get out of here!

Eddie hurried down the steps and shoved the quilt as

far back in the corner of the alcove as possible. At that moment, the lighthouse door opened. Eddie frantically looked for a place to hide. Suddenly he spotted the window by the banyan tree. Quickly Eddie climbed out onto the window's narrow ledge. The limb, which grew up to the window, looked sturdy so he grabbed it and swung out. The branch swayed wildly under Eddie's weight as he held on for dear life. Swallowing hard, he crawled along the limb like an inchworm until he reached the tree's massive trunk. Then he hid behind the branches until Mrs. Kimble passed by the window on her way to the lantern room. Rapidly he shinnied down the trunk and raced across the yard to the tool shed.

As soon as he unlatched the door, Rex jumped up and greeted him with a friendly lick on his face. Eddie hurriedly led Rex through the backyard, startling Lightning who jumped aside. Before the surprised rooster could crow, Eddie and Rex were already on their way to Duval Street.

Eddie noticed an old woman carrying a parasol coming towards them. He stopped and asked politely, "Excuse me, m'am. Do you know where the Key West Coffee Company is located?"

The woman gave him a piercing look. Then she replied sharply, "No I do not, but I do know where the school house is and you're very late this morning." Without another word, the lady rudely brushed past them.

"She's probably related to Frowny Browny," said Eddie under his breath.

He questioned people all along Duval Street until finally stopping to rest on a bench in front of a cigar factory. Several cigar rollers were smoking nearby. Eddie summoned his courage once more and approached the group of men.

"Does anyone know where I can find the Key West Coffee Company?"

A friendly man with a black mustache smiled and spoke in broken English.

"See man in store." He pointed down the street to an ice cream shop.

Eddie smiled, nodded his thanks, and called Rex. Together, they headed to the small ice cream parlor. When they arrived, Eddie told Rex to wait outside. Then he opened the shop's door and went in.

A man dressed in a white apron was working behind a long glass counter. A large mirror filled one wall of the store. When Eddie caught a glimpse of his reflection, he tucked in his shirt and tried to smooth down his unruly cowlick. The shopkeeper was thinly slicing something similar to bananas and then frying them. The savory smell made Eddie's stomach rumble.

"What can I get for you today, young man?" asked the shopkeeper looking up from his task.

All kinds of tempting frozen treats were displayed under the glass counter top. There were tubs of pastel-colored ice creams and fruit ices with flavors like mango and coconut.

"I'd like one mango ice cream cone and one bag of those," said Eddie. He pointed to the pile of fried chips the man had just dumped onto a piece of newspaper to soak up the grease.

"These are called *marquitas*. They're made from green plantains. People like them because they're so crispy."

Eddie reached deep into his pants pocket and pulled out some change from his silver dollar. He gave it to the shop owner who handed him the ice cream and a bag of chips.

"I'm looking for the Key West Coffee Company," said Eddie as casually as he could. "Would you happen to know where it is?"

"As a matter of fact I do," said the man. "I buy my coffee for the shop there."

Eddie's heart started to beat a little faster. "Could you give me directions, please?"

"Be glad to. It's not very far from here, but it's a bit tricky to find," said the shopkeeper. "Just stay on Duval until it runs into Front Street. Turn left and go down three blocks. The warehouse is located in a narrow alley that leads to a short dock."

Eddie thanked the man and left the shop. He sat under a palm tree near the ice cream parlor and put the bag of plantains down on the ground for Rex. At first the Lab sniffed suspiciously at the paper sack. Lured by the smell, however, Rex quickly tore the paper and started gobbling the chips. Eddie licked his ice cream cone as Rex continued to devour the plantains. When Rex finished, Eddie picked up the empty bag and tossed it in a nearby trash barrel.

"Let's go, Rex," said Eddie, wiping his sticky fingers on his pants. "The sooner we find the place, the better."

From the shopkeeper's directions, Eddie, with Rex at his side, finally located the alley. A crudely painted sign that said *Key West Coffee Company* was propped up near a crumbling cement wall of the building. Quickly, Eddie and Rex crossed to the other side of the street and hid behind a wooden fence. They did not have to wait long before the front door opened and Leo stepped out. After lighting a cigar, he leisurely headed for the dock.

Cautiously, Eddie and Rex followed him from a distance. He watched as Leo approached the dock and climbed aboard the sailboat with the navy blue jib.

Eddie whispered to Rex, "I wonder if the stolen payroll is still on board."

More than anything, he wanted to get his hands on one of the payroll bags, but it was just too dangerous. He'd come back tonight when Bart and Leo were fast asleep at the B'tween Waters Hotel.

Eddie and Rex hastily retreated to Duval Street and continued walking until they reached the lighthouse. Eddie felt better with each step away from the dock and the coffee company. He could hardly wait until school was out to tell Jen and T. J. what he'd seen.

From his perch in the banyan tree Eddie saw T. J. and Jen round the corner onto Whitehead Street a little after three o'clock that afternoon. Rex lay at the base of the huge tree, staring at the chickens on top of the coop. The Lab stood up and wagged his tail as T. J. and Jen opened the gate and went into their house. He ran to greet the twins when they came out and walked with them to the tree where Eddie waited. Then he took up his position again to watch the chickens.

"*¿Qué pasa?*" called T. J. scrambling up to the branch where Eddie sat. "What's going on?"

Jen followed close behind carefully placing her feet in notches that had been worn into the trunk by the twins' hundreds of climbs. She latched onto a strong branch to pull herself up the rest of the way.

"For starters," replied Eddie, "your mother almost caught me in the lighthouse today, but I crawled out that little window and hid in the tree."

"That was quick thinking," said T. J.

"I still think we should let Mother know about Eddie," Jen said to T. J., her brow furrowing as she spoke. "I don't like keeping secrets from her."

"You know we decided against that," argued her twin. "Besides, we'll tell her everything after Eddie gets a payroll bag . . ."

"I found the coffee company this morning."

T. J. and Jen immediately fell silent and turned their attention to their new friend.

"It's in an old building off Front Street," explained Eddie. "Bart and Leo are using the company as a cover for their theft operation. I talked to a shopkeeper who actually buys coffee from them. When I got there, I saw Leo and the sailboat with the navy blue jib. I'm sure the payroll is either on the boat or in the warehouse."

"You're a good detective," said T. J., with admiration in his voice. "When it gets dark, we'll go back there and you can get your proof at last."

"You'll go with me?" asked Eddie.

"Of course," said Jen. "We want to help."

"Just as soon as Mother leaves for choir practice tonight, we'll go," added T. J.

Later that evening Eddie, Jen, T. J., and Rex walked through the darkened town of Key West until they reached the narrow alley. Eddie pointed out Bart and Leo's sailboat which was bobbing in the water. Its navy blue jib whipped in the stiff Gulf breeze.

They crept over to the windows of the coffee company. Cupping their hands around their eyes, the three friends peered inside. No one was there.

"Jen," suggested T. J., "you and Rex stand guard near the door while Eddie and I take a look inside. Whistle if you see anyone coming."

Jen took Rex by the collar and hid nearby in the shadows while Eddie and T. J. both tried the front door.

"Maybe it's locked," said T. J.

"No," said Eddie. "I think it's just stuck. Help me."

Both boys put their shoulders to the jammed door. It opened and they tumbled into the warehouse. A dim light from the moon shone through the dirty windows. Cautiously, the boys began to look around. Suddenly the sound of fluttering wings broke the quiet and Eddie felt something brush against his face.

"Ugh . . . what's that?" he said, drawing in his breath sharply.

"It's a bat!" cried T. J.

The boys scrambled to get away as the bat swooped down again and then flew back to the rafters above them. In his haste, Eddie stumbled into a large trunk. Something metal crashed to the ground.

Jen stuck her head in the doorway. "What's all that racket?" she asked in a whisper.

"There are bats in here," her twin whispered back, "and Eddie's bumping into stuff."

"I've found a lantern," called Eddie from a dark corner, "and matches too."

"Light it quick," said Jen.

"I will," said Eddie. "You'd better get back to your post."

Jen nodded and went back outside.

As the wick caught fire, the small flame faintly illuminated the corner where Eddie stood. He raised the lantern high above his head for a better view.

"Look at that!" he said to T. J.

About twenty crates were hidden under a long counter stacked high with coffee bags. T. J. lifted the lid on one and reached inside. He pulled out a fancy goblet and then a shiny tray.

"Hey," he cried, "this looks like my Aunt Martha's silver platter!"

"Are you sure it belongs to her?" asked Eddie.

T. J. held the tray up to the lantern's light and turned it over to examine it more closely. "Yes, these are definitely her initials engraved on the back."

"I'll bet all this stuff is stolen," said Eddie. "Keep looking. Those payroll bags have got to be here somewhere."

Eddie moved slowly around the crates holding the lantern in front of him so he could see. Suddenly he noticed some canvas cloth stuffed between two crates. Before he could reach it, Jen whistled.

"Someone's coming!" warned T. J. "Put out the lantern and run."

Eddie and T. J. raced out the door and followed Jen and Rex in a mad dash down Front Street toward home. A raspy voice boomed from behind them, "Hey you brats! What are you doin'?"

Once they were on Whitehead Street, T. J. ran ahead and threw open the gate to the Kimble house. He and Eddie stood gasping for breath in the yard of the lighthouse. Jen crowded in behind them and sank to the ground breathing hard. Rex stretched out in the grass, panting to cool himself off.

"Whew," said Eddie, bending over to rest his hands on his knees as he gulped in fresh air. "Bart almost caught us."

His face was flushed as red as his hair. "I just wish I could have examined that canvas material."

"Well, one thing's for sure," said T. J. "It's too risky to go back to the warehouse tonight."

"Yes," agreed Jen when she finally caught her breath. "It's way too dangerous. No telling what Bart and Leo might do. Let's wait until morning. Then Mother can go with us to the police and they can handle it from there."

"Sounds good to me," said T. J. "I can identify Aunt Martha's silver platter."

"Eddie, will you be okay in the lighthouse one more night?" asked Jen.

"Sure," said Eddie. "I'll take care of Rex and see you in the morning."

The twins went into their house and Eddie put Rex in the shed. Then he wearily climbed the stairs to the little alcove that had become his home.

Eddie tossed and turned under the quilt. He kept thinking about the canvas cloth he'd seen between the crates. Could it be one of the F.E.C. payroll bags?

Then a disturbing thought crossed Eddie's mind.

What if Bart and Leo decide to move all the loot before morning? I've got to go back tonight!

Eddie hopped out of the alcove and quietly crept down the stairs. He hesitated a moment when he got to the Kimbles' gate. Then he turned and went back to the shed to get Rex. As he grabbed the Lab's collar to lead him through the yard, he thanked his lucky stars the chickens had all gone to roost.

"I could go by myself," he whispered to his faithful dog, "but I'll feel much safer with you along."

Rex jumped up and put his paws on Eddie's chest to lick his master's face.

"Okay, boy," said Eddie pushing Rex down and patting his head. "I know I can count on you."

The two started toward the Key West Coffee Company. It was late by the time they reached Front Street. Just as they turned into the alley, Rex began to bark. Suddenly an arm reached out and grabbed Eddie by his hair.

"Gotcha, you redheaded hooligan!"

7

West of Key West

"I knew you'd be back sooner or later," whispered Bart into his captive's ear. Eddie gagged on the smell of Bart's foul breath. "Me and Leo have been watching you real close."

At that moment Rex charged at Bart. The loyal canine clamped his teeth onto Bart's pants and tried to pull him away from Eddie. This time, however, Bart was ready. Using his iron-tipped boot as a weapon, the angry man kicked Rex squarely in the stomach. Rex yelped in pain and let go of Bart's pants. The violent man kicked him again and Rex went limp, his broken body sliding into the warehouse wall. Then he lay still.

"You killed my dog!" screamed Eddie. "You monster!"

Bart slapped his gigantic hand over Eddie's month and warned softly, "Shut up or you're next."

Turning to Leo, Bart ordered gruffly, "Dump that mangy mutt in them bushes at the end of the alley. Then git back here. We'll be inside."

Eddie watched helplessly as Leo grabbed hold of Rex's hind legs and started dragging his beloved dog away. He struggled to tear loose from Bart and get to Rex.

"That's enough!" said Bart roughly.

The huge man opened the warehouse door and shoved Eddie inside, throwing him onto the wooden planks like a sack of potatoes. Eddie's face hit the floor with a loud thud. Bart was right behind him and planted his boot on Eddie's back to pin him down. He tied Eddie's wrists together with a piece of rope; then grasping the ropes, he jerked Eddie to his feet. Bart smiled at the trickle of blood that ran from Eddie's lip.

The thief released Eddie long enough to strike a match and light the lantern. The single flame cast spooky shadows across the walls and Eddie scanned the rafters for bats. When he looked down, Bart was standing directly in front of him, an evil look on his face.

Eddie knew it was now or never. With all his might, he gave Bart's shin a swift kick and bolted for the door. While Bart yelled and hopped about on one leg, Eddie fumbled at the handle with his rope-tied hands. After several tries, it finally opened.

Leo stood waiting right outside. The wiry little man snatched Eddie and spun him around like a top. Then he marched the boy back inside the warehouse.

"Thought you'd git away from us again, did you?" asked Leo. "You're even stupider than I thought."

Bart's bearded face exuded hatred as he limped over to Eddie. He raised his hand and gave Eddie a sharp blow on the cheek. For a moment Eddie saw stars.

"Are you ready to cooperate now, boy?" growled Bart.

Eddie slowly nodded his throbbing head up and down.

"That's more like it," said Bart. "You should always respect your elders."

Leo added his two cents. "He's right, boy. To tell the

truth, me and Bart was surprised to see you in Key West. After that first time at the hotel, though, we knowed all along you was followin' us. We're glad you sought out our company. Yessir, it's a good thing because from now on you'll be our number-one employee."

Bart snorted. "Leo, you do have a way with words."

Leo grinned at the compliment. "Why thank you, Bart, kind of you to say . . ."

"Please," interrupted Eddie. "If you let me go, I won't make any trouble."

Bart snorted again and shook his head. "It's not that easy. If we set you free, you'll go straight to the police and sing like a bird. No way. You know too much. From now on, you're not going anywhere without us."

"Yessir," said Leo, "we're sticking to you like barnacles on a clam, like gum on a shoe, like . . ."

"Shut up, Leo," interrupted Bart. "You run your mouth too much. I've got a few things to say too. Git over here so's we can talk."

Bart and Leo huddled near the door and spoke in whispers. Meanwhile, Eddie anxiously looked for another exit from the warehouse, but the thieves were blocking his only means of escape.

I'm trapped. I can't even get a message to T. J. and Jen and there's no telling what those two men will do. . . . Just look at what they did to poor Rex.

At the thought of Rex, Eddie's eyes filled with tears. He squeezed them shut.

When Eddie opened his eyes, he saw Bart pulling a knife out of his belt and coming toward him. Eddie cringed and waited. To his surprise, Bart walked around behind him and cut off the ropes at his wrists. With his hands free, Eddie immediately rubbed his swollen cheek and wiped the blood from his lip with his fingers.

Then the large man hobbled over to the far side of the warehouse, still favoring his leg. He pointed to the crates of stolen loot that Eddie and T. J. had discovered earlier that evening.

"Load 'em onto the sailboat, boy," said Bart. "Leo's takin' first watch. If you're a smart lad, you won't give him no trouble."

Then Bart limped over to a string hammock that hung between two wooden posts. He climbed in and stretched out his considerable bulk. The hammock sagged dangerously close to the floor.

Leo pulled a shiny revolver from inside his coat and pointed the tip of the gun at Eddie's heart. "Don't stand there like a stick, boy," ordered Leo. "You've got work to do."

Eddie reached for a dolly and started loading it with crates, his heart pumping with fear. When the dolly was full, he slowly wheeled it into the dark alley. Leo walked directly behind him still brandishing the gun. Eddie dragged his feet on the way to the dock hoping against hope he'd see someone, but the lane was completely deserted. As they approached the sailboat with the navy blue jib, Leo pointed it out to Eddie.

"That's our sailboat. Yessir, she's a real seaworthy vessel."

Eddie saw the name, *Java Mugs*, painted on the side of the boat.

"Named it myself," said Leo proudly. "Clever, ain't it? The coffee or java company is a front for our robbery operation and naturally everyone thinks the mugs part means coffee cups, not thieves. Yessir, we advertise our illegal activities right on the side of our boat for all the world to see. Them police is too stupid to figure it out, though. It's a good joke, don't you think? Ha, ha. Why, only the other day . . ."

Eddie tried to block out Leo's constant babbling. He just wanted to finish his task to avoid the backside of Bart's hand again.

After rolling the dolly to the edge of the dock, Eddie picked up the heavy crate and carefully stepped on board. Leo was behind him still congratulating himself for giving the sailboat such an inventive name.

"Set it over there under that tarp," ordered Leo. "We like to keep our 'coffee' dry, if you know what I mean. Ha, ha."

Eddie set the crate of stolen goods down and then carried the other two onto the boat's deck. On his way back to the warehouse to get the next load, Eddie cut his eyes from side to side looking desperately for help. The minute Leo picked up on what he was doing, Eddie felt the gun in his back.

"Don't go thinkin' about runnin', boy," advised Leo, "or you'll be joinin' your dog in them bushes."

Eddie wheeled the dolly back inside the warehouse. Leo stood in the alley smoking a cigar while Eddie stacked his next load of crates. His mind raced as he desperately tried to think of a way to escape from his captors. Suddenly he remembered the canvas cloth he had seen earlier that evening. He paused, listening for Bart's steady snoring. Then Eddie located the canvas cloth, reached down, and pulled the material from between the two crates. Sure enough, it was a payroll bag with *Marathon* and the F.E.C. logo stamped on it! He opened the canvas bag and looked inside.

It's empty. Bart and Leo must have put the gold coins into the crates with the rest of the stolen stuff, but this payroll bag is all the proof I need. Somehow, I've got to get it to the police.

Eddie thought about stuffing the empty payroll bag in his shirt but it was too bulky and would soon be discovered by Leo's observant eyes. He searched for a safe place to hide it. Any minute Leo would come looking for him. Then Eddie spied a wide crack in the back wall of the warehouse. He hastily jammed the payroll bag into the crevice. Then he crossed the room and rolled the crate-filled dolly to the door.

Eddie made many trips from the warehouse to the sailboat. It was evident the two thieves had been stealing quite a lot lately. With every step Eddie pictured faithful Rex thrown into the bushes like a piece of garbage and it was all his fault. If only he'd waited for the twins to come with him, Rex might still be alive. Eddie was overwhelmed with guilt and grief, but he kept moving. He had to. Leo's gun was pointed at him every minute. Eddie concentrated on putting one foot in front of the other as he walked to the warehouse and back to the *Java Mugs*.

"Well, glad to see you're finally cooperatin'," said Leo with a smirk.

Eddie worked mechanically and kept his face expressionless so Leo wouldn't see the emotions that filled his heart. He only stopped to rest when the last crate was safely stashed on the bow of the sailboat. Eddie stretched his aching muscles. He rubbed the back of his neck and looked up at the sky. Rosy streaks of dawn were just beginning to color the horizon.

Eddie jumped a foot when Bart's harsh voice bellowed right behind him. "What are you waitin' for, boy?" he barked. "Git below! We're leavin'!"

Bart jumped on board the *Java Mugs* and pushed Eddie toward steps that led to the cabin below.

"Yes, sir!" said Eddie hurrying to obey.

"That's not fast enough," shouted Bart, kicking Eddie down the short flight of stairs.

Eddie pitched forward into blackness, hearing only the click of the key as Bart locked him inside the small cabin. He picked himself up from the floor and blinked several times before his eyes adjusted to the darkness. Suddenly a bird's screech came from inside the room. Eddie followed the sound and found a parrot sitting on a low perch.

"Have they kidnapped you too?" he asked scratching the bird's green feathers.

"Chico! Chico!" squawked the parrot hopping onto Eddie's shoulder.

"Chico? Is that your name?" Eddie asked. "Well, Chico, I guess you and I are going to be cell mates."

Eddie took Chico off his shoulder and set the noisy bird back on his perch. Then he stretched out on the cabin's bunk and closed his eyes.

"Quit squawking, Chico," said Eddie seriously. "I need quiet so I can figure out how to get out of this mess." He rolled over and faced the wall.

Who am I fooling? I'd better face the grim facts. There is no escape from this boat. We're already sailing out to sea. T. J. and Jen don't even know where I am. Pa's in jail and Rex is dead.

Exhausted and alone in the dark, Eddie finally let the grief take him and cried himself to sleep.

Eddie wasn't sure how much time had passed when he was awakened by Bart kicking his bunk. He sat up, rubbed his swollen eyes, and looked around. In the dim light, Eddie saw Leo sitting at a table in the small galley. Chico was still on his perch.

"We've just dropped anchor so git up and fix breakfast," ordered Bart. "There's hardtack and smoked bacon in the cupboard along with some fruit. Git to work!"

Leo hid his crooked teeth behind his hand as he snickered. "He's our galley slave now, right Bart?"

Eddie climbed off his narrow bunk and followed orders. He set out some raisins and pineapple on a plate. While Eddie worked, Leo reached over and swiped a raisin for Chico. The parrot plucked the raisin from Leo's fingers and swallowed it in one gulp. Then he began to fly around the room, stopping to peck at the glossy bald spot on Bart's head and his polished tin cup. Then Chico swooped down, snatched Bart's cup and carried it back to Leo, dropping it in his lap.

"Leave my cup alone, you obnoxious bird or I'll put you in the stew pot!" growled Bart, grabbing his cup from Leo.

"Don't say that, Bart," whined Leo. "You know Chico loves shiny things."

"Then keep that fool parrot away from me," he said, glaring at his skinny partner.

Leo meekly put Chico back on his perch. Eddie watched from the corner of his eye, taking in Leo's fear of Bart and Bart's fear of birds. Suddenly a smile started at the corners of Eddie's mouth. He bit his lower lip to keep it from spreading across his face.

These two thugs are cowards!

He tucked that bit of information away for future reference and felt his courage return. There'd be no more tears. Eddie Malone wasn't a crybaby and he wasn't giving up!

When Bart and Leo finished eating, they tromped upstairs to lift anchor and set sail again, leaving their kidnapped slave to clean up the dishes. Eddie quickly gobbled down some breakfast while Chico flew around the cabin pecking at the tin cups on the table and a mirror hanging over the tiny wash basin.

"Chico! Come, Chico!" called Eddie softly, holding out a raisin to the bird like he'd seen Leo do.

The parrot took the raisin and flew to his perch to eat

it. When Chico finished, Eddie gave him another one before stuffing the few remaining raisins in the pocket of his knickers. He didn't know when he'd get to eat again and he wasn't taking any chances.

"Boy!" Bart's scratchy voice startled Eddie. "Come here."

Eddie ran up the stairs. Bart was waiting for him on deck with a rag mop and a metal bucket filled with water.

"Swab the deck till it shines," he ordered. "Then mend them fishin' nets over there." He pointed in the direction of the bow. A pile of tangled nets spilled out from a big wooden box near Leo, who was aimlessly watching the seagulls wheel overhead.

Eddie took the mop and bucket and began scrubbing the filthy deck. Occasionally, he glanced up from his work and tried to get his bearings, but he only saw sky and water. As the hours passed, Eddie felt the hot sun burning his fair skin. He rolled his shirtsleeves down to protect his arms and wrapped his jacket around his head like a turban. He wished he had an aloe plant. Rubbing the aloe gel on a sunburn always made his skin feel better.

Eddie studied the position of the sun as it moved across the sky. The sailboat seemed to follow the direction of the sun so he knew they were heading west. He tried to remember facts from Frowny Browny's geography lessons on the Florida Keys.

In the late afternoon, Leo brought Eddie some water and hardtack. As Eddie stood at the rail to eat, the *Java Mugs* passed the remains of a wrecked ship sticking out of the shallow waters.

"We used to be in the wreckin' business," commented Leo. "When me and Bart found ships stranded on the reef, we'd go alongside and take all kinds of cargo aboard. Finders keepers we'd say. Then the competition got too fierce, so we switched to old-fashioned methods of stealing. Ha, ha!"

Suddenly Eddie caught sight of a big fort looming in the distance. It was a six-sided building made of red brick walls eight feet thick and fifty feet high. A black iron lighthouse rose up from one of the walls. The fort was surrounded by a moat which protected it from the pounding surf.

All at once Miss Brown's geography lesson came back to Eddie. He was at Fort Jefferson, seventy miles west of Key West! Miss Brown had said Fort Jefferson was a miserable place of blistering heat, disease-carrying mosquitoes, and utter isolation. The fort had been used as a prison and its moat cut off all means of escape. Eddie shuddered when he remembered that last fact.

The sun was setting as Bart maneuvered the *Java Mugs* to Fort Jefferson's long dock. Eddie stood on deck and gazed at the bright orange ball on the horizon. He made a wish.

I wish I may, I wish I might see the green flash tonight. I sure do need that luck T. J. was talking about.

There was no green flash that night, however. Eddie knew he'd run out of luck for sure when Bart kicked him down the stairs again and locked him inside the cabin. His heart dropped to his feet at the kidnapper's parting words.

"Enjoy your last night aboard the *Java Mugs*!"

8

Waiting Game

As Eddie felt his way through the dark cabin, he pushed back the fear that flooded over him like a giant tidal wave. When he reached his hard bunk, he crawled into it and lay down. Eddie laced his fingers behind his head and stared up at the low ceiling. If he just thought about it, surely he could outwit two stooges like Bart and Leo.

Just then, Chico swooped over from his perch. He landed on Eddie's stomach and started pacing back and forth.

"Hungry, Chico?" asked Eddie. The bird bobbed his shiny green head up and down so Eddie propped himself up on his elbows and fished some raisins from his pocket. He held one up between his fingers. Chico quickly snatched it with his beak.

"Life's simple for a parrot," observed Eddie. "You just eat and sleep."

As if to prove that point, Chico plucked another raisin from Eddie's fingers.

"Humans have it harder, Chico," continued Eddie, a hint of frustration creeping into his voice. "Why, look at Pa and me.

We're honest people. Bart and Leo, on the other hand, are not. Yet we're the ones who get locked up while those two mugs roam free. I tell you, Chico, life is for the birds."

When the raisins were gone, the fickle parrot flew back to his perch. He cocked his green head and stared at Eddie.

"Know what, Chico?" asked Eddie, lying back down. "I'm thinking if only Pa hadn't taken the job with the Florida East Coast Railway, then we wouldn't have moved to Marathon and I wouldn't be in this trouble right now . . ."

Eddie's voice trailed off into the silence of the cabin.

I shouldn't blame Pa. Getting kidnapped in Key West was my own fault, but what am I going to do now?

Eddie forced down the desperation that rose inside him like Matthew's weed in the tube. He covered his eyelids with his hands and tried to focus on solving his dilemma.

I'm scared and that's keeping me from thinking clearly. Sure, it looks hopeless, but still there must be something . . .

Suddenly Eddie opened his eyes and propped himself up on his elbows again. He looked over at Chico. "That's it!" cried Eddie. "Bart and Leo *think* they're smart, but they're really just bullies. You know what I'm going to do, Chico? I'm going to be patient and watch for my chance to outwit them!"

From his perch, Chico squawked excitedly and flapped his wings. He swooped around the dark, stuffy cabin several times before returning to his perch.

Voicing his declaration of independence aloud gave Eddie a renewed sense of confidence, the most he'd felt since Pa's arrest. He rolled onto his side and let the gentle motion of the sailboat rock him to sleep.

Friday morning, the clunking sound of Bart and Leo's heavy boots coming down the stairs broke into Eddie's peaceful dreams. When he looked around, Eddie saw Bart dangling a food bag over his bunk. "Fix our breakfast, boy, and be quick about it."

Bart and Leo moved to the galley's table. Chico flew through the cabin, finally resting on Leo's bony shoulder. Bart started impatiently drumming his fingers, so Eddie got to work. He hastily filled the cracked plates with dried meat, hardtack, and raisins. When the coffee had brewed, he poured it into the tin cups. While the two men were hunched over their food, Eddie quickly chewed some meat strips and washed them down with coffee. Then he slipped some raisins into his pocket for later. While Bart and Leo ate, they made plans for the day.

"Spike should get here from Cuba by this afternoon," announced Bart. "I sure hope that old salt remembered to bring the stuff I asked for. We can rest while the boy here loads Spike's coffee cargo onto the *Java Mugs* and then moves our crates aboard Spike's boat."

"Sounds good to me," agreed Leo. "By the way, where's Spike sellin' our loot this time?"

"He's sailin' up to Schaffer's Warehouse in Tampa and storin' the stuff there until the Key West police quit searchin'. When the coast is clear, he'll ship it by rail to the black market up north."

"What'll we do with the boy till Spike gets here?" asked Leo.

"Since you asked about him, you can watch him," answered Bart. "I'm plannin' on a siesta under those date palm trees outside the fort."

Leo frowned. "Do I have to?" he grumbled.

Bart just laughed again and lumbered away from the dock.

After handing Eddie the mop and bucket, Leo instructed him to keep an eye on Chico and make the parrot stay out of the water barrel. Then Leo ambled to the stern of the sailboat. He stretched out on the deck and put a large straw hat over his face to shield it from the sun. Chico fluttered around Leo's head a minute and then settled on the boat's mast.

Eddie mopped his way toward the bow. When he was out of Leo's sight, he laid the mop down and leaned on the railing to rest.

In spite of his situation, Eddie couldn't help admiring his surroundings. Being out on the water always lifted his spirits. He watched brown pelicans overhead as they coasted through a cloudless sky and then plunged into the blue-green waters, scattering a school of tarpon that swam through the coral reef. Fronds of the date palm trees rustled in the light breeze. Eddie liked the arches that formed the fort's red brick walls. They reminded him of the concrete ones he'd seen on the Seven Mile Bridge just south of Knight's Key.

Reluctantly, Eddie made himself go back to work. He deliberately moved the metal bucket closer and closer to the tarp-covered crates. Reassured by the snoring coming from beneath Leo's straw hat, Eddie reached over and folded the end of the tarp back.

If I could take one of those lids off, I'd be able to get a good look at some of the stolen things. Then I could describe them to the police . . . that is, if I ever make it back to Key West.

Eddie found a crate with a crooked lid and pried it off. He was astounded! On top was a delicate set of hand-painted china packed carefully in straw. Below the china were two silver candlesticks with bases entwined like snakes. Nestled in one corner was a small, octagon-shaped jewelry box covered with emeralds and rubies. Each object was more beautiful than the last, but Eddie still didn't see the gold coins from the F.E.C. robbery.

He carefully put the lid back in place. Just as he started to lift another lid to search the next box, a shadow fell across the crate. Eddie spun around with a start. Leo stood behind him with his arms folded against his chest. Chico flew down from the mast to sit on Leo's shoulder and began squawking.

"So you thought you'd just take a peek inside the crates while old Leo was nappin'," said the thief gruffly. "Boy, you're askin' for trouble and after you've loaded Spike's ship, you're gonna git it!"

Leo reached for the mop and shoved it into Eddie's hand. "Now git back to work before I really lose my temper."

Eddie did as he was told and returned to his task. As the day wore on, the merciless sun beat down on Eddie's back making him feel like it was on fire, but he was determined to finish the job. By the time Bart came back to inspect the deck, even he couldn't find fault with Eddie's work.

Later that afternoon, Eddie stood on the dock and watched a sailboat gliding toward the island. Finally the small boat pulled along side the *Java Mugs*. When the sailor climbed out of his boat and onto the dock, Eddie couldn't believe his eyes. The man looked exactly like a pirate. He wore a red and white striped shirt, black leather pants, and tall knee boots. He had tied his long black curly hair back with a piece of string and an eye patch covered his right eye. His most distinctive feature, however, was a gold ring encircled with tiny spikes that hung through his pierced nose.

"Bart! Leo!" boomed the pirate with a grin. "Your partner in crime has arrived and I'm ready to exchange goods."

Bart came up and slapped the big man on his back.

"Spike, you old seadog, it's about time you showed up."

Just then Spike looked over in Eddie's direction and frowned. "What ho! Who have we here?"

"Don't worry about that scallywag," said Bart with a wink. "After tonight, he won't be botherin' nobody, if you get my drift."

"Yeah," said Leo. "Good riddance. Right, Chico?"

Chico squawked and flew onto Spike's shoulder. The pesky bird leaned over and grabbed the ring in the pirate's nose with his beak. He held on with a fierce determination and began flapping his wings in an attempt to snatch the shiny object.

"Git him off me!" screamed Spike, trying to bat Chico away with his hands. "He's killing me!"

"Come, Chico, come," said Leo trying to coax the parrot back onto his shoulder. But Chico was infatuated with the gleam of the ring and wouldn't let go. Finally Leo caught the parrot with both hands and pulled him away from Spike's nose ring.

"Ow! Ow!" cried the pirate as he jumped around holding his bleeding nose.

"I told you to keep Chico on board," Bart muttered to Leo. "Now we're in big trouble. Spike already don't like the boy bein' here and now the bird's made a fool of him."

"It's the boy's fault," whined Leo pointing his tobacco-stained finger at Eddie. "That redheaded rascal was supposed to be watchin' Chico."

"Put that daffy parrot on the boat, Leo," said Bart sternly, "then git back here."

Spike dabbed blood from his sore nose with a dirty handkerchief and glared at Eddie. Then straightening himself up to his full height, Spike took charge and began barking orders.

"Don't just stand there gapin', boy. Unload my boat," he snarled, "and while you're at it, bring me that box of Cuban rum and cigars sittin' over there." He pointed to a wooden box sitting on top of some crates.

Once again, Eddie was forced to move cargo. First he brought Spike the box of rum and cigars. Then he started lifting the crates marked *Key West Coffee Company* from the pirate's sailboat onto the dock. The pungent fragrance of the coffee beans wafted through the wooden slats.

While Eddie worked, the three thieves sat leisurely on the pier and dangled their legs over the water. Spike opened the box and took out a big bottle of rum. Then he passed out cigars and soon the acrid smell of cigar smoke hung in the air. Their raucous laughter rang out as the dark golden rum disappeared from the bottle. From time to time, Spike looked over his shoulder to check Eddie's progress.

"Be extra careful with them small boxes on the port side, boy," warned Spike, slurring his words as he spoke, "or you'll blow us all to smithereens!"

Eddie's eyes widened with alarm as he read the word *dynamite* on several boxes that had been carefully stashed in a separate pile. Nervously, he brushed at his cowlick with sweaty palms. Then slowly and gently Eddie lifted the boxes one at a time. It was all he could do to keep his hands from shaking. Moving the dynamite with such care, however, gave Eddie a chance to hear snatches of the thieves' conversation.

"I hope you brung enough of the dynamite," said Bart, eyeing the little pile of stacked crates on the dock.

"Don't you worry none. There's more than enough to blow a big chunk in the tracks and stop that inaugural train. Are your plans all set?"

"Sure," said Leo, smiling his snaggletoothed grin. "This

is gonna be our biggest heist ever. First me and Bart will sail to the north end of Marathon and tie up in the mangroves there. Then we'll lay low till Sunday night. When it's good and dark, me and Bart will put the dynamite sticks under the tracks that cross the Vaca Cut to Marathon. Then we'll hide nearby until morning. When we hear the whistle from the Flagler Special as it passes through the Crawl Keys, we'll light the fuses, then . . . ka-boom!"

"Yeah," chimed in Bart, greedily rubbing his hands together. "The train'll be forced to stop in that deserted place. With nobody around to help them, those wealthy people goin' to the Key West celebration will be sittin' ducks waitin' to be robbed."

Stunned by what he'd just heard, Eddie almost dropped a crate. He quickly set the box down and wiped the sweat from his hands.

Eddie recognized the spot the thieves were talking about because Pa had been one of the workers building up the roadbed there with marl. Vaca Cut had been a creek that connected the lowlands of the Crawl Keys to the higher ground of Marathon. It was indeed a very remote spot and a good choice to pull off a train robbery.

Suddenly aware that Bart had turned around and was watching him closely, Eddie forced himself to slowly pick up the box of dynamite again and put it aboard the *Java Mugs*.

When the cargo exchange was finally completed, Spike hoisted himself up and mumbled, "Time's awastin'. I'm off to Tampa. You can git word to me at Schaffer's Warehouse."

The pirate handed Bart and Leo another bottle of rum and then staggered back to his sailboat. As the sun sank into the west, the three watched Spike sail away until his boat disappeared from sight. Eddie kept his eyes peeled for the green flash. It was somehow comforting to know that Jen and T. J. were watching for it too.

Suddenly Eddie felt the sharp jab in his back that sent him sprawling onto the dock. He picked himself up and turned around. Leo was holding his gun and waving it at him.

"Me and you is goin' for a little walk."

Pushing Eddie with the nose of his gun, Leo nudged him toward the moat's bridge. Out of the corner of his eye, Eddie caught sight of Chico hopping around near the box of cigars. Bart was timidly trying to shoo him away.

"Take this stupid bird with you," Bart called to Leo. "He's pesterin' me."

Leo called to Chico. Immediately, the parrot left Bart and flew to Leo's shoulder. Then the odd trio marched across the bridge into Fort Jefferson.

When they reached the fort's entrance, Leo and Eddie climbed the stairs to the second floor. At the top they turned left and continued along a narrow walkway to a small concrete room. An opening on the back wall let in a breeze from the Gulf. *Abandon hope all ye who enter here* had been written in black letters over the barred door.

"What's this?" asked Eddie hesitantly. The quote over the door didn't sound promising.

"Your new living quarters," said Leo, oozing with false sweetness. "Don't you worry none. You'll be as comfortable as the former resident, old Dr. Mudd himself."

Generating some false enthusiasm to stall for time, Eddie inquired, "Dr. Mudd? Who's Dr. Mudd?"

"He was a prisoner here in 1865," replied Leo. "He tried to escape, but he got caught. There's no escape from Fort Jefferson!"

"What did he do?" asked Eddie frantically looking

around for a board, a rock, anything to throw at Leo.

The scrawny man smiled his crooked grin and warmed up to his subject. "Why, Dr. Mudd set John Wilkes Booth's leg after Booth shot President Lincoln in the Ford Theater. You see, Booth broke his leg jumpin' down onto the stage to get away."

"Aren't doctors supposed to help people?" asked Eddie, keeping the conversation going.

"Well, yeah," answered Leo, "but Booth killed the president! Mudd was arrested. At the trial it came out that he knew Booth before the assassination, so Dr. Mudd was pronounced guilty and put in prison here. He finally got pardoned though."

"Why?" Eddie asked. For once, he hoped Leo would just keep talking.

The kidnapper took the bait and continued, "When a yellow fever epidemic broke out in prison, Dr. Mudd saved a lot of lives. Because of that, the President done gave him a pardon and set him free." Then Leo cackled, "A president's pardon is the only way out of here and you sure ain't gittin' one of those."

With that, Leo threw Eddie inside the cell and slammed the door. Then he took a key from a nail on the wall outside and turned it in the lock. With one last glance at Eddie, he returned the key to its hook and started down the stairs. Suddenly Chico flew to the shiny key and lifted it off the nail. Then he circled around Leo's head with it in his beak.

Leo grabbed the parrot by the neck and returned the key to the hook. Then he firmly set the bird on his shoulder and started back down the steps, scolding Chico all the way to the bottom.

Eddie walked to the small window and looked for the

Java Mugs. It was still at the dock, but the sight of Bart packing up to leave scared him more than anything he'd ever been through before. It had been awful when Ma had been dying, when Pa had been dragged off to jail, and when he'd seen Rex get kicked, but this was the worst of all. Now he was being left on this island . . . all alone to die.

9

East to Key West

Eddie stood helplessly in front of the cell window at Fort Jefferson. All he could hear was the roar of the surf and the pounding of his heart. He tried not to panic when darkness fell and the wind became his only companion.

Eddie sat down on the floor and dug deep in his pocket for the raisins he'd stuffed in earlier. He began popping them in his mouth one by one as he considered his predicament. The situation seemed hopeless.

Suddenly Eddie heard the flutter of wings as Chico swooped in through the window and then through the barred cell door to the walkway beyond. Eddie watched in amazement as Chico plucked the key from its hook and began flying around just outside his cell. Eddie immediately stood up, held a raisin between his fingers, and called softly, "Raisin, Chico, raisin."

The parrot flew into the cell and dropped the key to take the raisin from Eddie's fingers. Eddie bent down and snatched it up. Awkwardly, he reached through the bars to the lock on the outside and stuck in the key. With a single turn, there was a metal click and the door swung open.

Freed from his cell, Eddie ran down the stairs and crossed the bridge over the moat. He slowed his pace as he neared the *Java Mugs*. Anxiously he looked around until he saw Bart and Leo sprawled on the pier, their snores echoing over the open water. Another bottle of Spike's rum lay empty beside them. Quietly he snuck past the thieves and climbed aboard the sailboat.

Eddie crept toward the bow where he had stacked the crates earlier. He carefully pushed the boxes apart until he made a crawl space. Then he lay down and wedged his body between the crates. After covering himself with the heavy tarp, there was nothing left to do but wait in the darkness and pray he would not be discovered.

After a fitful night, Eddie woke to the sound of waves slapping against the hull as the sailboat raced through the water. Slowly, he shifted his cramped body under the tarp to find a more comfortable position. He desperately wanted to leave his hiding spot but that was out of the question.

Eddie, be patient. You're on your way home to Marathon. All you've got to do is wait . . . and hope Bart and Leo don't find you!

Eddie's stomach protested with a growl. He checked his pockets, but he'd given his last raisin to Chico. As the morning wore on, the sun began to beat fiercely down on the deck. In the stifling heat, Eddie felt like a Florida lobster in a steam pot. He had to get some fresh air. Cautiously, Eddie lifted the edge of the tarp a few inches and let his eyes adjust to the daylight. The first thing he saw was the wooden floor he'd mopped so clean. Then he spotted it. There on the deck just a few feet away lay the key to Dr. Mudd's cell!

Yikes! Chico must have pulled the key from the lock and

brought it here. I've got to get that key before Leo or Bart sees it.

Eddie stretched his arm out from under the tarp and reached for the key. It was too far away. He rolled onto his stomach and slid a little closer. When the boat tipped to the left, he stretched farther and looped his little finger through the hole in the top of the key. Just then, Chico flew down from the mast and clamped his beak around the key's opposite end. Caught in a tug-of-war, Eddie tried to pull it away from Chico. The stubborn bird, however, refused to let go and flapped his wings wildly.

Eddie heard Bart's grating voice in the distance. "Leo, see what Chico's worked up about and make him stop."

At the sound of boots approaching on the planks, Eddie let go of the key and pulled his arm back under the tarp. He scarcely breathed as he listened to Leo's voice.

"What ya got there, Chico?" Eddie heard the clink of the key on the deck and knew Leo had seen it.

Then Eddie heard Leo muttering to himself. "Chico must have doubled back to the cell and picked it up, unless somehow the boy got it. . . . No, no Leo. You locked him up. There's no way that he could have gotten out of that cell. Still, that boy's a tricky one. . . ." Then Eddie heard him walk away.

Oh, no. Now Leo's suspicious. If he starts looking for me, this tarp will be the first place he'll check. Chico knows I'm under here and could make trouble too. I'd better find a new hiding spot.

For the next few minutes, Eddie wracked his brain trying to think of another hiding place on the small boat. Then he remembered the wooden box nearby where Bart and Leo stored fishing nets. If he could just get in there, he'd be safe. Bart and Leo wouldn't be fishing on this trip. They were too busy planning their train robbery.

Eddie lifted the tarp and peeked at the sun overhead.

Noontime. He knew Bart always took a siesta between noon and two o'clock. He waited for a few minutes until he was sure Bart was in the cabin below. No doubt Leo was at the wheel but as long as Eddie kept down low, he would be out of Leo's line of sight.

Slowly, Eddie emerged from under the tarp and crawled on his hands and knees like a baby until he reached the box. When he opened the lid, Eddie discovered it was filled to the brim with fish nets. Hastily, he pulled out several bulky nets and shoved them next to the water barrel. Then he crawled in and stuffed some fish net between the box and the lid. After lowering the lid over himself, Eddie rested his head near the crack he'd made with the nets. Now, at least, he had some air and could even see a little bit of the deck. Eddie pulled his knees up to his chin and waited, lying on the scratchy nets.

Soon loud voices alerted Eddie that Bart's siesta was over. Peeking through the crack, he saw Bart strolling toward him. Eddie held his breath when the big man stopped right in front of the box.

"Leo, get over here," called Bart. "I've told you time and time again to put the fish nets away so's I don't trip over them."

Leo came straight away and stood beside Bart looking down at the tangled heap.

"But I didn't leave the nets out," argued Leo. "I'm sure I put them away."

"Well, do it again," said Bart sarcastically. "Maybe this time they'll stay in their place. I'll even hold the lid while you put them away, *again*."

Eddie felt a whoosh of air as the lid was thrown open. He squinted up into the bright sunlight and Bart's ugly face. Bart's expression of surprise rapidly changed to one of anger as he pulled the frightened boy out of the box.

"Leo! How did this redheaded troublemaker get aboard?" demanded Bart, twisting Eddie's arms behind his back. "I thought you locked him in Dr. Mudd's cell."

"I did, Bart, honest I did," said Leo worriedly.

"Well, he ain't there now, is he?" said Bart in a low, menacing voice.

"No, Bart, he sure ain't.

"So what do you think we should do?" asked Bart.

"I don't know, Bart."

"Would you like to know what I think, Leo?"

"Yes, Bart, I would," said Leo, nodding his bony head up and down.

"Well, I think we should throw somebody overboard," said Bart slyly.

Leo's face turned white and he shrank away from Bart.

Bart looked at the little man and shook his head with disgust.

"Not you, you idiot," said Bart. "The boy."

Eddie struggled to get loose, but Bart held onto him tightly.

"You got nowhere to run, nowhere to hide," said Bart with a nasty sneer. "Time to go to your watery grave."

The two kidnappers lifted Eddie up and tossed him overboard like a rag doll. The last thing he heard as he flew through the air was Bart's cruel laugh.

With a loud splash, Eddie hit the cold water and went under. When he surfaced, he started treading water. Any hope Eddie had of the thieves changing their minds vanished with the *Java Mugs* as it sailed out of sight. He swung his head from side to side looking for land or at least something he could latch onto to keep afloat. Eddie loved swimming but even he couldn't survive in the water forever.

He began talking out loud to boost his courage.

"Calm down, Eddie. Just keep your head up and think."

Reassured by his own advice, Eddie carefully searched the horizon once more. There was nothing but ocean as far as the eye could see in front and to the sides of him. As Eddie slowly treaded water, he turned his body around to look behind him. About two miles away, rising up from a coral reef, was the square iron tower of the Sand Key Lighthouse!

Frantically Eddie began swimming west toward the small island. Each pull of his arms took tremendous effort against the strong current and suddenly he realized he was caught in an undertow. He stopped fighting the current and swam sideways until he no longer felt the ocean pushing against him. Then he started swimming toward the lighthouse again. Sometimes he'd flip over on his back and float a while to rest.

Eddie felt himself slipping into a dream world as he struggled to keep going. It would be so easy to give up and drift down to the soft sandy bottom of the ocean. He could sleep forever with the loggerhead turtles and the lavender sea anemones.

If only the dolphin that saves people would come around . . . but T.J. said Angelina was just a silly legend. Still it couldn't hurt to try.

Eddie's last conscious thought was of calling the dolphin's name. "Angelina! Angelina! Angelina!" he whispered into the seawater that filled his mouth. Then the waves washed over him and he sank beneath the surface of the water.

* * *

The next thing Eddie felt were the gentle swells of the ocean lifting his body onto the hard-packed sand. Slowly he opened his eyes and looked up. The Sand Key Lighthouse loomed over him. When Eddie found the strength to sit up, he stared out at the sea. Later he would swear to all who would listen that he had seen a beautiful gray dolphin leap from the water and smile at him as it flipped its tail in a goodbye wave. Eddie Malone had become a believer in legends.

He stood up on wobbly legs and limped to the lighthouse. Then he forced himself up the steps to the keeper's quarters and knocked at the door. No one answered so Eddie used both his fists and pounded hard. There was still no answer. It was then that he noticed a pencil and pad hanging on a hook by the door. The note said, "Medical Emergency. Gone to Key West. Be back Tuesday. Charles Johnson, Lighthouse Keeper."

Eddie collapsed on the platform of the keeper's quarters. It seemed that every time he got a break, he ran into another brick wall. He was just plain tired of fighting.

Tuesday! I can't wait that long! I have to get the payroll bag in Key West and get to Marathon by tomorrow night, so I can prevent the train robbery.

Suddenly through cracks between the wooden planks, he caught sight of a small sailboat hanging in the eaves beneath the platform. Eddie took the pencil from the doorframe and scribbled on the bottom of Keeper Johnson's note. "Borrowed your sailboat. Will leave it at end of alley off Front Street in Key West. Thanks. Eddie Malone."

Eddie scrambled down the stairs and untied the ropes to lower the boat to the sand. A rush of energy fueled by hope quickened his fingers and soon he had the boat in the water. He raised the sail and was on his way. When he spotted the Key West Lighthouse, he set his sights on it and aimed for land. An ocean breeze pushed the little skiff closer and closer to shore until at last, Eddie reached the dock near the Key West Coffee Company.

Once ashore he tied up the sailboat and raced toward the warehouse through late afternoon shadows that crept across the road like long, skinny fingers. When he reached the alley, Eddie stopped running and cautiously approached the warehouse. At the front of the building he peeked through one of the dirty windows. No one was there. Eddie opened the door and stepped inside.

A number of empty crates were scattered about the room and Bart's old string hammock still hung between the wooden posts. Eddie made a beeline for the back wall. He stuck his hand inside the crevice to retrieve the payroll bag. He felt all along the crack— but it was empty!

10

Riding the Rails

Once again, Eddie ran his hand along the crack in the warehouse wall. The result was the same. The payroll bag was gone. He searched through all the old crates, but it was nowhere to be found. His frustration left a bitter taste in his mouth and Eddie angrily kicked an empty crate across the room. Then he sat down on the floor and put his head in his hands.

At that moment he discovered he was not alone after all. Eddie let out a shriek and jumped up as an enormous rat skittered across his foot. The hairy rodent scurried into a hole in the baseboards of the back wall. Then he saw it. A piece of canvas was sticking out of the hole.

Eddie broke off a plank from a crate. Warily, he squatted down near the opening. Using the wooden board, he carefully eased the canvas sack out of the rat's nest and carried it over to the window. The rat had chewed a hole in it, but the F.E.C. logo and the word *Marathon* were still intact. Eddie clutched the payroll bag to his chest. Finally he had something concrete to show Sheriff Jenkins!

All at once the fatigue he'd been holding at bay finally hit him. Exhausted from his adventures at sea, Eddie crawled into Bart's old hammock. After cushioning his head with the payroll bag, he closed his eyes.

I'll just rest for a few minutes. Then I'll go to the docks and wait for the Montauk *to arrive. Since it's the only steamer to Marathon on Sunday, I must get on it if I'm going to stop Bart and Leo. Maybe I can . . .*

Suddenly the shrill sound of the *Montauk's* whistle pierced the air. Eddie sat up and opened his eyes. Rays of sunlight were streaming through the dirty windows above him. It was morning and he was still in the warehouse!

Eddie scrambled out of the string hammock. He grabbed the payroll bag and bolted for the door. He paused for a moment to secure the canvas bag inside his shirt. Then he rushed into the alley and ran toward the docks.

A Sunday morning church bell pealed in the distance calling people to worship as seagulls squawked overhead. Crowds milled through the streets, enjoying the fine January morning. Eddie, however, ignored the sounds and sights around him. He was in a race against time.

He darted in front of a horse-drawn ice wagon, forcing the driver to swerve sharply. The startled man angrily shook his fist, but Eddie didn't see him. He was too busy weaving through a family with four children who were out for a leisurely stroll around town.

When Eddie dashed by an old woman walking two white poodles, the dogs yapped wildly and strained on their leashes. By the time he reached the dock, Eddie realized he was too late. The *Montauk* was just a speck on the bright, sunny horizon.

Sweating and breathing hard, Eddie plunked down on a bench.

If I had just slept here last night instead of the warehouse, I would have been able to catch the steamer. If only I'd . . .

Eddie shook his head to stop the negative thoughts.

Quit it, Eddie. You've managed to escape from the kidnappers, to get to Key West, and to find the payroll bag. Don't give up now!

Even the waves that slapped against the dock's pilings seemed to be saying, "Think, think."

I might be able to persuade a fishing boat captain to take me to Marathon.

Eddie knew that idea would not work. Even if a captain agreed, he didn't have enough money to pay.

Maybe I could find someone with an airplane, but that's unlikely. Even if I did, flying is dangerous and expensive.

Eddie knew he was grasping at straws, but he was desperate.

Then an idea struck him like a ton of bricks.

The survey train!

Eddie thought back to the conversation he'd overheard between Pa and Miss Brown. A survey train was to test the tracks to Key West on Sunday, January twenty-first.

Why, that's today! At this very moment, the survey train should be on its way here to Key West. If I could sneak on that train when it goes back to Marathon, I could be home by tonight.

Excitedly, Eddie jumped up from the bench and hurried to the nearby railway station. When he got there, he caught a glimpse of himself in one of the station's windows. He was shocked to see how messy he looked. Hastily, he ran his fingers through his unruly red hair. Then he tried to smooth out the wrinkles in his jacket and knickers. It was no easy task because his saltwater swim had made his clothes stiff and smell like fish. When he felt somewhat more presentable, he approached a friendly-looking woman with a basket. She was giving out big sugar cookies to her two young boys.

"Excuse me, ma'am," said Eddie politely. "Are you here to see the survey train?"

"Why yes, young man," replied the woman. "It should be coming into the station any time now. My boys begged me to bring them to the station. They just couldn't wait until tomorrow to see a real steam engine."

At the sight and smell of the cookies, Eddie's stomach growled loudly. He blushed deeply and said, "Excuse me, ma'am."

The kind woman smiled and reached into her basket. "Here, young man," said the woman putting three cookies into his hand. "Take these. They should tide you over until suppertime."

While Eddie ate, the talkative woman continued to chat with him. Her husband worked with the F.E.C., so she knew quite a bit about the Over-Sea Railroad.

"The railroad took seven long years to complete. Imagine. Why just today, the last spike was driven completing the Over-Sea Railroad! As we speak, the survey train is barreling down the tracks. I hear tell that Mr. William Krome and Mr. C. S. Coe are riding on it. They're Mr. Henry Flagler's chief engineers, don't you know. Mark my words, young man, history is being made right before our very eyes!"

Eddie nodded as he finished the cookies. He thanked the lady and then wandered over to join a few other curious spectators on the platform. At last he heard the whistle announcing the survey train's arrival.

Eddie watched the coal-burning locomotive rumble into the station, its black steam engine belching smoke like an angry dragon. Finally the powerful train screeched to a halt under a large wooden water tank.

While a few onlookers admired the train, Eddie quickly

slipped across the tracks. He passed the brakeman who was busy polishing and cleaning the headlight. Eddie glanced over each shoulder. Then he hid behind a bushy plant while the train crew loaded coal and water into the tender, the car attached directly behind the steam engine. When the servicing of the train was finished, the engineer hopped into the cab and blasted the whistle. The fireman checked the boiler and gave a nod to proceed. The spectators backed away from the tracks as the powerful steam locomotive roared to life.

Eddie knew this was his chance. Like a streak of lightning, he sprang from his hiding place and climbed into the very back of the tender. As he lowered himself into the car, coal dust poofed into the air and settled all over his hair and clothes, giving Eddie an idea. He picked up a piece of coal and blackened his face and neck too. It was the perfect camouflage to protect him from the fireman's watchful eye. Then he wriggled down into the coal for the ride back to Marathon.

Eddie stayed hidden until they crossed the first bridge. Then he peeked over the top of the tender to see the view. He watched dolphins in the waters below as they raced the train. Maybe one of them was Angelina. From his high perch he could see different hues in the water. In some places it was brown. Eddie knew that meant reef formations and seagrass were close to the surface. White meant shallow water and sand bars. The deeper waters were blue and green. That's where large boats went to fish for amberjacks, groupers, and tarpon.

Every time the train came onto another Key, Eddie ducked back deep into the coal to keep from being seen. He scrunched down as low as he could and waited impatiently until the train was traveling over the sea again.

As the hours passed, Eddie grew more and more anxious. Did he have enough time to get to Marathon and find the sheriff? Could he convince the sheriff of Pa's innocence this time? Would the sheriff believe he was telling the truth about Bart and Leo's plot to rob Henry Flagler's train? A lot depended on him and time was running out.

It was dusk when the survey train finally chugged into Marathon and pulled to a halt. There were cheers from below as the huge locomotive and tender stopped under a coal bin. Just then, a big metal arm swung over the tender and huge chunks of coal started rumbling down the chute. Eddie scrambled out of the car and leaped to the ground. He rolled over in the sand, stood up, and started running down the track. He hadn't gotten far when a commanding voice rang out. It was the train's fireman.

"Hey you!" he shouted. "Stop where you are!"

11

Race for Time

Ignoring the fireman's order to stop, Eddie kept running as fast as he could away from the train station. He paused and checked over his shoulder a minute later. No one was chasing him, so he took off running again. He hoped he wasn't too late to stop Bart and Leo. The only way to find out was to get to the Marathon jail as fast as possible.

Eddie held the payroll bag tightly to his chest and raced through the town. When he reached the water barrel, he paused to dip some water to quench his raging thirst.

Then he removed his jacket and turned it inside out. After pouring water over his head, he used his jacket to wipe the coal dust from his face and hands. Then he tied the jacket at his waist and headed straight to the jail.

Bursting into the sheriff's office, Eddie removed the canvas bag from under his shirt and threw it on the sheriff's desk. "Here's my proof," he panted. "Now you've got to let my pa out of jail!"

"Whoa!" said Sheriff Jenkins. "Slow down, boy. What are you talking about?"

"Don't you remember?" asked Eddie impatiently. "I'm talking about Frank Malone. He's locked up back there. You said he stole last week's F.E.C. payroll."

"Oh, you're his son, aren't you?" said the sheriff. "Look, I told you the last time you came in here that I've got an eye witness who has identified Frank Malone as the thief. Not only that, but your pa's fingerprints were found all over the paymaster car."

"I know it looks bad for Pa," said Eddie, "but now I've got proof it was those two thieves I saw on Sand Dollar Key. They stole the payroll."

Eddie picked up the bag and pointed to the word *Marathon*.

"See," he said. "This is one of the payroll bags that was stolen last week. I found it in Key West at the thieves' warehouse along with lots of other stolen stuff like silver and jewelry."

Sheriff Jenkins frowned and scratched the back of his neck as he studied the bag. Eddie could see he'd gotten the man's attention.

"Well, I don't know," said the sheriff doubtfully.

"There's more," said Eddie, seizing the opportunity to press on. "Those thieves are going to blow up the tracks before the train gets to Marathon tomorrow. Mr. Flagler's train will be forced to stop and then they'll rob the passengers."

The sheriff's head jerked up at the mention of Mr. Flagler's name. His eyes narrowed and he locked his gaze on Eddie's face as he leaned towards him.

"If you're lying, boy, I'll put you behind bars with your old man," growled the lawman. His face was so close that Eddie could smell onions on the sheriff's breath. Eddie swallowed a gulp and stepped back a little.

"No, sir," he said. "I'm not lying. I heard it with my own ears after they kidnapped me in Key West."

Eddie chewed on his bottom lip and nervously pulled at his cowlick. Then he looked the sheriff in the eye.

"I'm telling the truth," Eddie said. He made an "x" over his heart with his index finger. "Cross my heart and hope to die."

"Maybe you'd better start at the beginning," said Sheriff Jenkins, his eyes boring holes in Eddie's face. He reached in his drawer and pulled out a pencil and tablet.

"Now let's hear it," he ordered. The words tumbled out as Eddie bravely told his story. He tried to keep the details in order, but sometimes he had to go back and add things he'd forgotten, like how Bart tried to catch him in the lighthouse. Eddie told the sheriff all about Bart and Leo's theft operation. He also told him about Spike taking the stolen goods to Schaffer's Warehouse in Tampa.

From time to time, Sheriff Jenkins asked Eddie questions, but mostly he made notes. When Eddie finished, the sheriff leaned his chair back on its rear legs and stared at the ceiling as he considered Eddie's story. Suddenly the chair dropped to the floor on all four of its legs and the sheriff stood up. He began to pace around the office, his hands clasped behind his back. Eddie bit at his fingernails as he waited for the sheriff's decision.

Finally the sheriff stopped his pacing and spoke. "I'll ring my friend Sam at the police station in Key West and see if he knows anything about this."

The sheriff walked over to a telephone that was mounted on the wall and lifted the receiver off its hook. "While I'm making this call, you go on back and see your pa."

As Eddie walked to Pa's cell, he listened closely to what

Sheriff Jenkins was saying to the Key West police. The lawman was joking with the person on the other end of the line.

When Eddie got to Pa's cell, Frank Malone was asleep on the cot. He'd flung his arm over his face to block out the light from the bare bulb that hung from the ceiling. Moths flitted around it making thumping noises as they hit the glass.

"Pa!" Eddie called softly through the bars. "It's me, Pa!"

Frank Malone lifted his arm from his face and turned his head toward Eddie. Then he sat up.

"Eddie?" he asked. Quickly he got off his cot and walked to the cell door.

"Pa!" cried Eddie. "I've got some real proof from Key West that should get you out of jail."

Frank Malone's eyes widened in surprise. "You what?" he asked.

"Sheriff Jenkins is calling the police in Key West right now," said Eddie, pointing to the front office. "Maybe we can hear what he's saying."

Eddie and Pa fell silent as they listened to the sheriff's conversation. "Well, Sam, here's the reason for my call. We've got us a situation here that needs checking on. Ya see . . ."

The sheriff gave a detailed description of Eddie, red hair, cowlick, and all. Then he read from his notes. When the sheriff finally stopped speaking, Eddie peeked around the corner to see what he was doing. The sheriff was holding the receiver at his ear and appeared to be listening intently.

"The Key West police are talking to him now," whispered Eddie as he came back to the cell bars. Then he tiptoed back to the corner to listen again.

Every now and then, the sheriff would say, "Uh, huh" and "I see." Finally, the sheriff said, "Well, thanks Sam. I'll keep you posted."

Eddie hurried back to his pa's cell as Sheriff Jenkins rang off and placed the receiver back on the hook. Then the lawman walked down the hallway to Frank Malone's cell.

"Well, your son's story holds up," said the sheriff addressing Frank Malone. "The Key West police said a Mrs. Kimble and her twin children had reported the kidnapping of your son. The young 'uns said they'd been with Eddie when he found the Key West Coffee Company warehouse filled with crates of stolen goods. The boy, T. J., even recognized a platter that had been taken from his aunt's house. He saw what he thought might be a payroll bag, too."

The sheriff continued, "Evidently, some thieves have been stealing from well-to-do families in Key West. The police down there have some good leads. Now with the information your son has provided along with the Kimble children's testimony, the police are confident that the case will soon be solved."

"Pa, isn't that's great news?" cried Eddie.

Frank was stunned with all he'd heard. He tried to speak, but no words came out. He could only nod his head.

Then Sheriff Jenkins bent down until his face was level with Eddie's.

"The Key West police think I should check out your story about the thieves blowing up the tracks," continued the sheriff. "I agree."

"Let's go," said Eddie urgently, starting for the door. "If we hurry, we should be able to find Bart and Leo."

"You be careful, son," called Frank Malone through the bars. "I don't like you gittin' near them two kidnappers again."

"I'll watch out for him," assured Sheriff Jenkins. "If your son's got this right, you'll be released by day's end."

For the first time since the arrest, Eddie watched Pa's eyes fill with hope. Then before Eddie could even wave goodbye to Pa, the sheriff hustled him out into the night.

"Come on, boy," ordered the sheriff. "I've got to round up a few men to help us and then we'll be on our way."

Eddie and the sheriff hurried through the streets of Marathon, passing the water tower and the new recruits' tent camp where Eddie and Pa lived. When they got to the dining hall, the sheriff approached three railroad workers who were playing poker on the screened porch.

"I need a posse right now," he said motioning to them. "Come with me."

The men dropped their cards and followed the sheriff and Eddie outside.

"This boy here says two thugs are fixing to blow up the train tracks," the sheriff explained. "If it's true, I'm going to find and arrest them so I'm deputizing you all. The Key West police say these two men are dangerous, so be on your toes tonight."

When the group got near Adderley Town, Eddie saw the path to Matthew's house. He wished he could ask for Matthew's help too, but there was no time. The posse quickly crossed to the train tracks and followed them east out of Marathon. As they approached the Vaca Cut, the sheriff ordered them to split up. He and Eddie fanned out a little to the left of the tracks. The other men did the same on the right side. Up ahead they could see a faint light flickering.

The sheriff directed Eddie to stay put. Then the lawman drew his gun and started picking his way over the rocky embankment where two shadowy figures stood bent over the tracks.

When the sheriff got closer, he pointed his gun directly at Bart and Leo and shouted, "Stop in the name of the law! Put down that dynamite and get your hands up in the air."

The startled robbers carefully laid the dynamite at their feet and raised their hands over their heads. The posse rushed in to assist the sheriff. Two men held the thieves at gunpoint, while the third man carefully put all the sticks of dynamite back into the box. The sheriff took out two sets of handcuffs and snapped them onto Bart and Leo's wrists.

"Now march!" ordered the sheriff waving the two thieves back toward Marathon with his gun. The three deputized men surrounded Bart and Leo to keep them from escaping.

Just then Chico flew out of some bushes, attracting the attention of everyone.

The parrot circled around the group of men several times before coming to rest on Eddie's shoulder. When Bart saw Eddie, he became enraged and yelled out, "Why you redheaded . . ."

Before he could say another word, the sheriff gruffly ordered, "Shut up and move along."

Bart scowled and lumbered beside his partner Leo, who for once, managed to hold his tongue.

When the group arrived back at the Marathon jail, the posse waited in the office with Bart and Leo. Chico flew off Eddie's shoulder and perched on the coat rack in the corner. He started pecking at the brass buttons on the sheriff's coat while Eddie followed Sheriff Jenkins back to Frank Malone's cell.

"Thanks to your son's efforts, you're free to go," said the sheriff letting Pa out of the cell. "I apologize for the mistake and I'm grateful to your son for helping me capture the *real* payroll thieves."

Eddie and Pa moved away from the jail door so the men could bring Bart and Leo in. Without a moment's hesitation, Sheriff Jenkins shoved the robbers inside the cell and slammed the door shut.

"You two will be behind bars for quite a long spell!" said the sheriff as he twisted the key in the lock. "I'll notify the Tampa police to pick up Spike. He shouldn't be hard to spot with that ring in his nose. Then I'll put in another call to Key West to update them on the situation."

Eddie and Pa quickly walked through the sheriff's office to the door. As they passed by the railroad workers, one of them started clapping and soon the whole posse joined in. They each thanked Eddie and took turns shaking his hand. The young hero's face turned as red as his hair, but a huge grin stretched from one corner of his mouth to the other. Frank Malone smiled at Eddie's embarrassment, but his fatherly pride was evident. He patted Eddie on the back and said, "Let's go home, son!"

"What about this bird?" called Sheriff Jenkins who was trying to pull his jacket away from the parrot.

Eddie looked back at the sheriff and smiled. "His name is Chico and he's partial to raisins." Then he and Pa quickly exited the building.

On the way home, Frank Malone stopped and put a hand on Eddie's shoulder. "Eddie Malone, you done made me proud. You set your mind to freein' me and never looked back. If your ma were here right now, I know she'd be proud too."

Then Pa looked around him. "Hey! I don't see Rex. Where's he gotten to?"

Eddie just shook his head, unable say anything. He looked down and started making circles in the dirt with the toe of his shoe. Frank stood quietly and waited for Eddie to speak. Finally the words tumbled out.

"Rex is dead," said Eddie softly. "Bart killed him."

Without saying a word Frank held out his arms and Eddie walked into them. The son buried his head in his father's chest.

"Go ahead and bawl," said Frank. "When a man loses his dog, it's a time to cry."

At long last Eddie felt safe. He cried until he had no more tears. Then raising his head, he sniffed a couple of times and wiped his nose on his sleeve.

"I'd like to eat, wash up, and then get some sleep," said Eddie.

"Good idea," said Pa. "We could both stand a bath and some decent vittles. Then you can sleep as late as you want. There'll be no school tomorrow. Everyone will be down at the station in the morning to wave at the Flagler Special as it passes by."

After they washed up and ate, Eddie got into his cot and pulled the covers up to his chin. He was asleep as soon as his head hit the pillow.

Suddenly Eddie was startled awake. Someone was pounding on the screen door of the tent!

12

Key West Extension

"I'll get the door, Pa," volunteered Eddie. He jumped out of bed and padded barefoot across the rough floorboards. The first rays of sun were just beginning to shine through the canvas walls of the tent. Remembering the sheriff's recent visit, Eddie cautiously opened the door. A tall man wearing a Florida East Coast Railway uniform stood on the steps.

"Are you Eddie Malone?" inquired the man politely.

Eddie answered in a timid voice. "Yes, sir. I am."

Looking relieved, the man said, "I'm sure glad I found you. There isn't much time."

Without further explanation, he handed Eddie a stiff white envelope stamped with the official F.E.C. logo on it. *Master Eddie Malone* was scrawled across the envelope in black ink.

"Pa," called out Eddie, "it's a letter. . . ."

Pa walked to the door and acknowledged the stranger with a nod. Then he glanced over Eddie's shoulder and studied the fancy script.

"Well, son," said Pa, "since the letter's addressed to you, why not open it?"

Eddie struggled with the flap. Finally he eased the thick paper from the envelope. After clearing a frog from his throat, Eddie read the letter aloud.

January 22, 1912

Dear Master Malone,

Your efforts to aid the Florida East Coast Railway have just been brought to my attention. In appreciation for your loyalty to the F.E.C., I am inviting you and your father to ride on the Extension Special to Key West this morning. As my guests, all expenses will be paid, including food and lodging. If this arrangement is satisfactory, the porter will escort you and your father to the train within the half hour.

Cordially,
Henry M. Flagler

Eddie looked up from the letter, his eyes round as saucers. "Mr. Henry Flagler, the famous railroad builder, wants *us* as his guests?"

Frank Malone shook his head in disbelief. "You never know what the day will bring. Do you want to go, Eddie?"

"I sure do," exclaimed Eddie, "but only if you come with me, Pa."

"Are you kiddin' me, boy? After workin' day and night in the marl pit for Mr. Flagler, I'd be right honored to go."

"Hooray!" shouted Eddie. "Let's ride the rails together on the Extension to Key West!"

The porter waited outside the tent while Eddie and Pa quickly got ready for the trip. Eddie washed his face and brushed his teeth. Pa combed his hair and trimmed his beard. Then they put on the best clothes they had. While

Pa laced up his boots, Eddie packed a duffle bag. Pa picked it up and together they followed the porter to the train station.

When they got there, a large crowd was waving and cheering on the platform. Five passenger cars, filled with many important people, were linked together behind the massive steam engine and its tender. Mr. Flagler's private green-colored railcar, *Railcar No. 91*, was coupled to the very end of the train.

The porter took Eddie and his pa to one of the passenger cars and they climbed aboard. Then the porter walked down the crowded aisle until he reached the only two empty seats left on the train.

"Gentlemen, these seats have been reserved for you," he said with a smile on his face.

Pa thanked the porter and let Eddie scoot in first so that he could have the window seat. Eddie opened the passenger car's window and leaned out to wave at the people. Pa moved closer to the window too. At the edge of the platform stood Frowny Browny with Eddie's entire class. Even the occasional rain showers hadn't dampened the spirits of his classmates as they cheered the train with their teacher. The stunned look that swept across Miss Brown's face when she saw Eddie waving from the window made him laugh out loud.

Then Eddie surveyed the crowd until he found his old friend, Matthew Lawrence, standing with his wife. Eddie yelled to him. Matthew's face lit up like a Christmas tree when he saw his young friend sitting with his father on the special train.

A whistle blasted and thick smoke billowed from the locomotive into the rainy morning air. The crowd at Marathon moved back when the train pulled away from the station. Sounds of the cheering throng echoed in Eddie's ears as the Extension Special chugged south on the shiny steel tracks.

Eddie marveled at the sensation of riding on top of the water. He could hardly believe he was back on the train again. This time, however, he was riding in style. As they rode through the lower Keys, the sun peeked out from behind the clouds. He and Pa watched as the skies began to clear. Pa kept leaning over to the window to breathe in the fresh ocean breezes. After being cooped up in jail for a week, Pa was enjoying his new-found freedom. Eddie knew exactly how he felt. He too was glad to be free again.

The train was in the middle of the Seven Mile Bridge when Pa spoke.

"Eddie, I done told you this already but I got to say it again. I'm proud of you. Goin' after them two thieves was a big risk and I know you done it for me. Thank you."

Eddie hugged Pa and then leaned back into the plush train seat to savor his father's words of praise. Just then, the porter came down the aisle. He leaned down to speak with them. "Mr. Flagler would like a brief word with both of you. If you would just come with me . . ."

Eddie and Pa got up and followed the porter through the swaying cars toward the rear of the train. Several guests looked up with interest and watched the tough-looking man and his young boy being escorted to Mr. Flagler's private quarters.

When they reached *Railcar No. 91*, the porter held open the door so Eddie and Pa could enter the luxurious room of the famous Standard Oil and Florida East Coast Railway baron. The first thing Eddie noticed was the rich oak paneling. The floors were covered with dark maroon carpet and fancy blue curtains with gold tassels hung at the windows.

The porter led them to a distinguished-looking old man sitting in a wicker armchair. His hair was snowy white and he had a white mustache. His eyes, although clouded by age, still held a hint of the unusual violet-blue color that had always been Henry Flagler's most notable feature.

"Mr. Flagler, sir," said the porter, "may I present Mr. Frank Malone and his son, Eddie."

The aged railroad builder invited them to sit down. Then looking at Eddie, he said, "I want to thank you personally, young man, for your heroic act. Thanks to your quick action, we are on schedule today to Key West. Most importantly, the passengers will enjoy a safe ride."

Then facing Frank Malone, Mr. Flagler continued, "Mr. Malone, I understand that when you were seen trying to apprehend the payroll thieves, you were falsely accused of the robbery and thrown in jail. I apologize for the misunderstanding. Both you and your boy are to be commended for the way you handled yourselves throughout the unfortunate ordeal.

"Now that the terminal in Key West is open," said Mr. Flagler, "I need some honest men to run the day-to-day operations there. Mr. Malone, would you be interested in a dock supervisor position? The work is steady, the hours are regular, and you'd be getting more pay. You'd also have more time to spend with your fine son here. What do you say?"

Frank Malone looked over at his son. When Eddie enthusiastically nodded his head, Mr. Malone replied, "Great. I think Eddie, here, likes the idea too. I'd be right proud to keep workin' for the Florida East Coast Railway."

"Consider it done," said Mr. Flagler.

After thanking the railroad builder for his kindness, Frank Malone and Eddie started to leave. Mr. Flagler called Eddie back for a moment and motioned for him to come close. He pressed a gold coin into the boy's hand.

Then he whispered into Eddie's ear, "The moving pictures will be showing in town. I think you and your father might enjoy seeing them."

"That would be swell. Thanks, Mr. Flagler," said Eddie, "and I want you to know that I really like your Key West Extension. It *is* the Eighth Wonder of the World!"

Mr. Flagler chuckled softly and sent Eddie on his way.

Back in the passenger car, Eddie and his father started discussing their move to Key West. Eddie could hardly wait to find Jen and T. J. and tell them the news. Their adventures together had forged a new friendship that would last a lifetime, but he wouldn't forget his old friend either. Eddie knew he would see Matthew when he came to Key West to sell his sponges.

As the Extension Special entered Key West, Eddie could feel the excitement in the air. He stuck his head out of the window and saw red, white, and blue bunting on buildings as far as the eye could see. When he shaded his eyes with his hand, Eddie located the lighthouse in the distance. He grinned at Mrs. Kimble's streamers atop the tower billowing out in the steady Atlantic breeze.

Ten thousand people were on hand to greet the train and join in the festivities. Conchs, the name given residents of the Keys, were joined by people of many other nations. Flags were everywhere. Cuban flags fluttered beside Old Glory as everyone milled around Trumbo Island waiting for the train's arrival. People held small American flags in their hands and shouted wildly. The chorus of one thousand school children lined up on the bleachers, ready to sing patriotic songs. Some of the children carried bouquets of brightly colored flowers.

Tents had been raised all over Trumbo Island. Church

ladies ran back and forth serving baked ham and pork sandwiches to the crowds who had come to view the historic event. Other items featured on the menu were guava pie, coconut ice cream, turtle stew, crawfish enchilada, conch chowder, and of course the island favorite, Key lime pie. Wooden wine barrels filled with a chilled mixture of Key lime juice and sugar syrup stood ready to quench the thirst of all who had gathered for the day.

The Light-Guard Band began to play a lively arrangement of "Dixie." A man dressed in an Uncle Sam suit with a blue top hat, followed behind them playing his flute. The beat of the drums and blare of the trumpets gave a military air to the whole celebration.

The man in front of Eddie pulled out his pocket watch. Then he turned to Eddie and said, "For the rest of your life, you'll always remember that at ten forty-three A. M. on January twenty-second, nineteen-twelve, you arrived in Key West on the Over-Sea Railroad."

"Yes, sir," said Eddie, looking out at the tremendous crowd. "I'll remember this day forever."

With one last burst of steam and a final blast of its whistle the Extension Special screeched to a halt in the terminal on Trumbo Island. Eddie and Pa followed the man with the watch down the steps and around to the back of the train.

The mayor of Key West, J. N. Fogarty, climbed onto the observation platform of *Railcar No. 91*. A hush fell over the crowd as they watched the door to Mr. Flagler's railcar open. When the grand old man, Mr. Henry Morrison Flagler, stepped onto the platform, the noise of their applause rose to a deafening pitch.

When the crowd quieted, the mayor welcomed Mr. Flagler and thanked him for the great contribution he had made to Key West and all of Florida. After the mayor's speech, a man stepped forward and presented Mr. Flagler with a gold and silver plaque from the residents of Key West. Then Mr. Flagler was given another tablet engraved with words of appreciation from the workers who had built the Key West Extension. The honored guest gave a short speech after receiving each gift.

Then friends accompanying Mr. Flagler assisted him from the train's platform and started walking through the crowds and past the bandstand where the children were singing "The Star Spangled Banner."

As the large group of dignitaries made their way to the red-carpeted stairs of the speaker's stand, Mr. Flagler paused for a moment and asked with a smile, "Do I smell roses?"

"Indeed you do," answered his friend. "The children have strewn your path with petals."

"I can hear the children, but I cannot see them," the old man replied. He greeted the boys and girls in the bandstand with a wave and listened to their happy voices lift in song. Eddie felt proud as he and Pa walked a few paces behind Mr. Flagler with all the other guests from the Extension Special.

As he marched along, Eddie stood on his tiptoes trying to find Jen and T. J. in the large choir. Suddenly a familiar howl floated over the strains of "Yankee Doodle." Eddie shook his head in disbelief. He pushed his way through the crowd until he could clearly see the faces of the children performing on the bandstand. Eddie quickly spotted Jen and T. J. standing together on the end of the front row. Then he gave a whoop of joy. Sitting at the feet of his friends, happily howling along with the chorus, was his faithful dog, Rex!

Eddie rushed to his dog's side. A large bandage was wrapped around the Lab's rib cage. Overcome with happiness, Eddie buried his face in Rex's yellow fur.

"Rex!" Eddie whispered in the dog's ear. "I thought you were dead, but here you are. Alive and well!"

Rex gave a yelp and stood up on his hind legs, his tail wagging as fast as it could go. He put his front paws on Eddie's chest with such force that he knocked his master to the ground. Eddie laughed and tried to keep Rex's friendly licks from covering his face. Finally Eddie managed to stand up and speak to T. J. and Jen.

"How'd you get here?" asked Jen, her eyes wide with surprise. "We thought you'd been kidnapped!"

"I *was* kidnapped," answered Eddie shouting to be heard over the singing.

"Well, we want to hear all about it!" T. J. shouted back.

The director of the children's chorus looked over at the three and glared. He kept directing with one hand and gave them the shush sign with the other.

"Follow us," said T. J. grabbing Jen's hand and ducking around to the back of the bleachers.

Eddie and Rex were right behind them. It was difficult to talk over all the singing, but Eddie had to find out about Rex.

"I thought Bart had killed him," said Eddie as loudly as he could.

"He almost did," shouted Jen. "We found Rex in some bushes the next morning when we went to the warehouse to look for you. He was really hurt bad, but Mother bandaged him up."

"Yeah," said T. J. "We told her everything. After that, she tried to help us find you, too. Then we went to the police."

"We can't talk anymore now," said Jen, glancing back at the chorus director. "Meet us at the lighthouse banyan tree after the speeches and we'll give you all the details."

Then Jen put her hands on her hips and tried to frown at Eddie. "I was really worried about you, Mr. Malone. You'd better be able to explain where you've been for the last five days."

"Sure," said Eddie, his lips parting in a wide grin. "I'll tell you all about it later."

The twins returned to sing with their classmates while Eddie and Rex headed over to the speaker's stand. Suddenly Eddie stopped and called to the twins.

"That's my pa!" he hollered, pointing with pride to Frank Malone who stood on the stage with Mr. Flagler and the other honored guests.

T. J. gave him a thumbs up sign and Jen smiled until both her dimples showed.

As Eddie and Rex stepped on stage beside Pa, a look of astonishment crossed Frank Malone's face.

"Rex?" he asked hesitantly. "Is that you?"

"It's a long story, Pa," whispered Eddie with a smile.

Pa reached down and affectionately patted the dog's head. Then Rex stood between them contentedly leaning against Eddie's leg.

"We've made it through some tough times," remarked Pa.

"And now we're back on track, aren't we?" said Eddie with a grin.

Frank Malone laughed at Eddie's pun and nodded his head in agreement. "Yep. Thanks to you, we're definitely back on track!"

Historical Notes

Big Pine Key: The beginning of the Lower Keys. As its name suggests, Big Pine has many pine trees. The trees make its landscape very different from that of the Upper Keys. Few people lived on Big Pine during the building of the Key West Extension. A thin layer of fresh water lies above the salt water under Big Pine Key. Construction engineers took the water from this layer and made a freshwater pond. Then they built ditches and tanks to transfer it into a huge one-hundred-thousand-gallon tank that had been built in the middle of Big Pine by railroad workers in 1906. This source helped supply some of the fresh water needed for building the Key West Extension project.

Cigar factory: A building where cigarmakers hand-rolled cigars. In 1868, the Cuban Revolution began and many Cubans fled to Key West and worked in cigar factories. By the late 1870s, Key West had over one hundred cigar factories in operation, annually producing one hundred million cigars.

Clarence Stanley (C. S.) Coe (1866–1939): A Florida East Coast Railway engineer who oversaw construction of a number of projects for the Over-Sea Railroad including Knight's Key Dock, the housing camp on Pigeon Key, and the Seven Mile Bridge.

Conch: Pronounced "konk." A name used to describe a resident or native of the Florida Keys. Many Key West residents refer to themselves as Conchs.

Coral reef: A narrow ridge of coral (small living organisms grouped together) that is near or at the water's surface. Found in subtropical and tropical waters, the reef-building corals grow very slowly. Coral reef formations in Florida can be found along the coasts of both the Atlantic Ocean and the Gulf of Mexico.

Cuba: An island ninety miles south of Key West, Florida. Havana, the capital city of Cuba, was a favorite destination of American tourists seeking Cuba's culture, weather, nightlife, and tropical scenery. Henry Flagler built his railroad to bring vacationers and freight from the north down the eastern coast of the United States to Key West. From there, a ferry took both travelers and exports to the nearby island of Cuba. When their country was at war in 1868, many Cubans fled to Key West and worked in cigar factories there. They brought their language, music, food, and architecture with them, adding a rich Spanish flavor to the southernmost city of the United States.

Dr. Samuel A. Mudd (1833–1883): A country doctor who became well-known for assisting John Wilkes Booth. Dr. Mudd lived on a farm in Maryland, not far from Washington, D.C. He sympathized with the south during the Civil War and belonged to the Confederate Underground. Because of his connection to John Wilkes Booth, the Confederate who assassinated President Abraham Lincoln, Dr. Mudd was convicted of conspiracy to kill Lincoln and sentenced to life in prison at Fort Jefferson. In 1867 an epidemic of yellow fever broke out at Fort Jefferson. As the fever spread, Dr. Mudd tirelessly helped the ill and dying.

Because of his great humanitarian efforts, President Andrew Johnson pardoned Dr. Mudd in February 1869 and he returned to his wife and children in Maryland. Throughout the years Dr. Mudd's family has worked to clear his name and historians still debate the question of Dr. Mudd's innocence. Was he just a country doctor helping a patient or was he a co-conspirator in President Lincoln's assassination?

The Dry Tortugas: A cluster of seven coral reefs that lies seventy miles west of Key West in the Straits of Florida, the narrow channel connecting the Atlantic Ocean and the Gulf of Mexico. The Tortugas were discovered by Ponce de León in 1513. The Spanish explorer named them Las Tortugas (The Turtles), but sailors later changed the name to Dry Tortugas because the islands have no fresh water. Green, loggerhead, and hawksbill turtles can be found here.

Florida East Coast Railway (F.E.C.): A railroad company owned by Henry Morrison Flagler. Flagler helped Florida's population grow by building a rail system and resort hotels along Florida's east coast. By 1912, the F.E.C. extended from Jacksonville to Key West.

The Florida Keys: A chain of small islands located at the southern tip of Florida. They stretch 150 miles from the mainland to Key West. The Keys are bordered by the Atlantic Ocean on the east and the Gulf of Mexico on the west. The chain of Keys is divided into the upper, middle, and lower regions. The Upper and Middle Keys are made of the skeleton of an ancient coral reef. Our nation's largest living coral reef lies east of Key Largo, the largest island in the chain. It is now called John Pennekamp Coral Reef State Park and is the only underwater park in our hemisphere. Pieces of egg-shaped limestone rock called Miami oolite form the Lower Keys. This geological structure holds a narrow layer of fresh water close to the surface.

Fort Jefferson: An army fort located on Garden Key in the Dry Tortugas that was part of a master defense plan to control navigation to the Gulf of Mexico and to protect ships bound for the Atlantic from the Mississippi River. During the Civil War the Union used it as a prison for military deserters. Fort Jefferson's isolation, lack of fresh water, mosquitoes, and intense heat made it the worst of prisons. Tradition holds that "Abandon hope all ye who enter here," a quote from Dante's *Divine Comedy*, was written over the door of the mess hall and one of the guardrooms. Dr. Samuel Mudd was its most famous prisoner. The fort was abandoned by the army in 1874, and in 1908 it was made a wildlife refuge for sooty terns. Today it is Dry Tortugas National Park and, though reachable only by boat or seaplane, it offers snorkeling, swimming, saltwater sport fishing, underwater photography, and a tour of the fort.

Green flash: A scientific phenomenon. Though seldom seen, the green flash happens at sunset when part of the sun suddenly changes from red to orange to green just before the sun completely disappears below the horizon. The change lasts only a second or two so has been called a "flash." It is caused by refraction, the bending of a ray of light as it passes at an angle through the atmosphere.

Henry Morrison Flagler (1830–1913): A business tycoon who made his fortune as a founding partner in the Standard Oil Company. In 1878, Flagler traveled to Florida and took an active interest in the state. He began building resort hotels for out-of-state visitors. He also bought the Florida East Coast Railway line and built railroads down Florida's east coast. Hoping to attract the shipping trade from Central and South America and Cuba, Flagler decided to extend his railroad line to the deep ports of Key West. The U.S. government was planning to build the Panama Canal and Flagler reasoned that Key West would be an ideal place to take in trade from the west after the canal was opened. From 1905 to 1912, Flagler supervised the building of the Key West Extension, also known as the Over-Sea Railroad, which connected the mainland through the Florida Keys to Key West by rail. He rode across the Key West Extension in his private railcar and arrived in Key West on January 22, 1912. In 1913, Flagler died at the age of eighty-three after suffering complications from a fall at Whitehall, his mansion in Palm Beach, Florida.

Joseph R. Parrott (1859–1913): Worked side-by-side with Henry Flagler as his general manager. He was responsible for hiring Howard Trumbo to create land for the Key West train terminal. In 1909, Parrot was named president of the Florida East Coast Railway while Flagler stayed on as chairman of the board.

Key deer: Tiny creatures about thirty-six inches tall that are a subspecies of the Virginia white tail deer. Sometimes they are called "toy" deer. They are great swimmers and will swim from one Key to another in search of water or solitude. About two-thirds of the three hundred Key deer in existence live in the refuge on Big Pine Key and No Name Key. Key deer are on Florida's endangered species list.

Key West: The southernmost city of the United States, located at the end of a chain of coral islands called the Florida Keys. Its tropical foliage and weather are similar to that of nearby Cuba and the Bahamas. In its early years it was a haven for pirates. Henry Flagler chose Key West as the final destination of his Over-Sea Railroad. Though it lacked adequate supplies of fresh water in the early 1900s, Key West boasted a cultured society of churches, a hospital, a school, a naval station, a ten-man police force, an electric plant, and many fine homes. Key West is a deep-water port and many steamships stopped at Mallory Docks on their way to New York or Cuba. It was customary in Key West for boys to dive for coins that passengers aboard the ships threw into the water.

Key West Extension: The 128-mile extension of Henry Flagler's Florida East Coast Railway System from Miami to Key West. Sometimes called the Key West Extension, the Over-Sea Railroad, Flagler's Folly, and the Eighth Wonder of the World, the railroad was a masterpiece of engineering that rivaled the Panama Canal in size and construction. It cost millions of dollars to build and provided hundreds of jobs. Some of those dedicated workers lost their lives while building the railroad. Construction began in 1905 and the Extension opened in 1912. The Over-Sea Railroad lasted twenty-three years.

In 1935 a monster hurricane struck the Keys and washed away forty-two miles of the railroad bed. After the hurricane, the F.E.C. received permission from the federal court to abandon the railway extension. Then the Overseas Road and Toll Bridge District, the State of Florida, and Monroe County bought all the bridges and rights-of-way and built the Overseas Highway on the track bed of Flagler's railroad. Now automobiles instead of trains travel the highway and bridges from Miami to Key West.

Key West Lighthouse: Built to replace the first lighthouse in Key West, which was destroyed by a hurricane in 1846. The eighty-six-foot lighthouse, built inland in 1847, is constructed of brick. A large banyan tree grows beside the lighthouse. The keeper's quarters were also built on the grounds. This lighthouse guided ships through the dangerous reefs around Key West. Visitors to Key West can climb up the eighty-eight steps inside the tower and view the city from the top of the lighthouse.

Knight's Key Dock: A man-made island of wood. The dock served as a place for Flagler's railroad to transfer supplies from ocean ships to barges for delivery to construction sites throughout the Keys. Knight's Key Dock had a warehouse with an office and depot. From 1908 to 1912 the dock was the southernmost terminal for moving people and cargo to and from ocean steamers and the F.E.C. Railway System. Tracks ran on either side of it to accommodate two trains and two ships at the same time. After the Key West Extension was completed, the dock could not be reached by train so it was burned to the waterline.

Marathon: A town located in the Middle Keys. Marathon was formed by connecting Little Hog Key, Knight's Key, and Key Vaca with fill. Marathon served as a center for boats and floating factories which supplied materials for the construction of the Knight's Key–Little Duck Key Bridge and the Bahia Honda Bridge. Henry Flagler wanted a major station and rail yard in the Middle Keys, so Marathon became the heart of the Key West Extension. Marathon started as a small camp in 1906 and grew into a town with a weather tower, a hospital, warehouses, a water tower, a post office, a general office from which Krome directed the Key West Extension project, a fish house, a hotel, tennis courts, and a school. A branch off the main train track shaped like the letter Y (called a wye) was built on the section that had been Key Vaca so trains could turn around and return to Miami. At times fifteen hundred men could be found working in Marathon. This fact gave rise to the saying that the town got its name from the "marathons" of men who lived there and worked for the F.E.C. Between the Key Vaca section of Marathon and Boot Key lies Boot Key Harbor. It is made up of marl, the best material for building roadbeds. The marl pit provided more than ten percent of fill for the Key West Extension.

Marl: A lime-rich, claylike mud with marine shell fragments in it. This valuable material was found in marl pits in the waters of the Keys. Workers removed the marl from the pit and used it to strengthen the roadbeds of the train tracks. After a few weeks, the marl hardened into a hard rocklike limestone.

Over-Sea Railroad: Another name commonly used for the Key West Extension.

Pigeon Key: A small island located approximately two miles west of Knight's Key. The Seven Mile Bridge that crosses Pigeon Key connects it to Knight's Key Bridge to the north and the Moser Channel Bridge, the Pacet Channel Viaduct, and Little Duck Key to the south. Pigeon Key's five acres were used to house workers constructing the bridges and to store cement. C. S. Coe moored his houseboat at Pigeon Key and his wife and children lived there with him at times. Pigeon Key had more than four hundred men and a few women living on it during the years when most of the bridge building was taking place. It had a large mess hall, dormitories, a bakery, a tent hospital, a cement warehouse, and a few small cottages. A generator provided electricity. Several buildings from the original camp are still on Pigeon Key and visitors are encouraged to ride a shuttle from the small museum housed in a train car on Knight's Key over to Pigeon Key on the only segment of Flagler's railroad that has not been replaced by the Overseas Highway. The remaining track bed sits high over the water and passengers can recapture the feeling of riding Henry Flagler's Eighth Wonder of the World in 1912.

Sand Key Lighthouse: A beacon built on a coral reef located nine miles southwest of Key West. The original Sand Key Lighthouse, constructed in 1827, was destroyed in the hurricane of 1846. A new lighthouse, built in 1852–53, was made of wrought-iron pilings that were bored into the coral reef. Thousands of terns nested on the small, sandy island that surrounded the lighthouse. Visitors to the island started gathering the tasty eggs and the bird population began to decline. In the early 1900s, lighthouse keeper Charles G. Johnson was hired as a warden to protect the nesting terns.

Sponge harvesting: Collecting sponges from shallow ocean waters. From around 1840 to 1870, sponging was a big industry in Key West. Often, two men would go out in a boat and look for sponge beds using a glass-bottomed bucket. A long pole with curved tines at one end was used to hook the sponge and pull it up. After pounding the sponges with a bat to remove any animal matter from the tough, elastic skeleton, the men would wash the sponges in seawater and string them up to dry. On land, the strong-smelling sponges were bleached and sold immediately.

Tortugas Harbor Lighthouse (Garden Key Lighthouse): Built in 1876 to replace the Garden Key Lighthouse, this hexagonal tower was constructed on one of the walls of Fort Jefferson at Garden Key in the Dry Tortugas. It was made of black, boilerplate iron and was first lit in April 1876. In 1921, the official use of the Tortugas Harbor Lighthouse was discontinued.

Trumbo Island: An area of 134 acres of man-made land used for Flagler's train terminal in Key West. The project's head engineer, Howard Trumbo, had marl and mud pumped up from the floor of the Gulf to create new land. Trumbo Island, the name used for Flagler's terminal complex, had a pier which was seventeen hundred feet long so that steamships could dock by it. When a train arrived at the Key West terminal, it could pull up alongside the ship. Train passengers could then get off the train, walk a few feet, and climb aboard a ship bound for Havana, Cuba.

William J. Krome (1876–1929): An engineer who worked for the Florida East Coast Railway as a surveyor looking for possible routes for the Key West Extension. Later, he worked closely with James C. Meredith, the construction engineer in charge of the Over-Sea Railroad. When Meredith died suddenly, Krome took over as the chief engineer and completed the Key West Extension project for Henry M. Flagler.

Wrecking: A large salvaging industry from the 1820s to the 1850s in Key West. When ships with valuable cargo would damage their boats on the shallow-water reefs, citizens from Key West would get in boats and go out to save the crew and the cargo. The salvaged items would then be put on auction. Many people in Key West made their fortunes from wrecking and by the 1830s, Key West was known as the wealthiest city, per capita, in America.

Here are some other books from Pineapple Press on related topics. For a complete catalog, write to Pineapple Press, P.O. Box 3889, Sarasota, Florida 34230-3889, or call (800) 746-3275. Or visit our website at www.pineapplepress.com.

Escape to the Everglades by Edwina Raffa and Annelle Rigsby. Based on historical fact, this young adult novel tells the story of Will Cypress, a half-Seminole boy living among his mother's people during the Second Seminole War. He meets Chief Osceola and travels with him to St. Augustine. (hb)

Escape to the Everglades Teacher's Activity Guide by Edwina Raffa and Annelle Rigsby. The authors of *Escape to the Everglades* have written a teacher's manual filled with activities to help students learn more about Florida and the Seminoles. Includes references to the Sunshine State Standards.

The Treasure of Amelia Island by M.C. Finotti. These are the ruminations of Mary Kingsley, the youngest child of former slave Ana Jai Kingsley, as she recounts the life-changing events of December 1813. Her family lived in La Florida, a Spanish territory under siege by Patriots who see no place for freed people of color in a new Florida. Against these mighty events, Mary decides to search for a legendary pirate treasure with her brothers. This treasure hunt, filled with danger and recklessness, changes Mary forever. (hb)

Blood Moon Rider by Zack C. Waters. When his Marine father is killed in WWII, young Harley Wallace is exiled to the Florida cattle ranch of his bitter, badly scarred grandfather. The murder of a cowman and the disappearance of Grandfather Wallace leads Harley and his new friend Beth on a wild ride through the swamps and into the midst of a conspiracy of evil. (hb)

Solomon by Marilyn Bishop Shaw. Young Solomon Freeman and his parents, Moses and Lela, survive the Civil War, gain their freedom, and gamble their dreams, risking their very existence on a homestead in the remote environs of north central Florida. (hb)

A Land Remembered: Student Edition by Patrick D. Smith. This well-loved, best-selling novel tells the story of three generations of the MacIveys, a Florida family battling the hardships of the frontier, and how they rise from a dirt-poor cracker life to the wealth and standing of real estate tycoons. Now available to young readers in two volumes. (hb & pb)

Hunted Like a Wolf: The Story of the Seminole War by Milton Meltzer. Offers a look at the events, players, and political motives leading to the Seminole War and the near extermination of a people. (hb)

Florida's Great Ocean Railway by Dan Gallagher. The incredible story of the building of the Key West Extension of the Florida East Coast Railway from Miami to Key West from 1905 to 1916, told with clear, engaging text and nearly 250 old photographs, many taken by the engineers themselves and most never before published. (hb)